THE FALLEN RING

THE COSMIC COLLECTOR

KEY DAWKINS

ALSO BY KEY DAWKINS

The Fallen Ring Series
The Fallen Ring (Book 1)
The Fallen Ring: A New Nemesis (Book 2)

ISBN: 978-1-7396186-6-7 (Paperback)

ISBN: 978-1-7396186-7-4 (eBook)

CONTENTS

When you learn to harness the power of your fears, it can take you places beyond your wildest dreams.

Jimmy Iovine

Prologue

The Martian dust swirled across the barren landscape, obscuring the approach of a metallic figure as it made its way towards an ancient ridge. Eradax's eyes glowed crimson against his iron-like exoskeleton as he studied the terrain. His body—a fusion of alien metal that resembled polished steel—reflected the dim sunlight while he crouched at the edge of a massive crater.

'The entrance must be here,' he muttered, his voice a mechanical rasp that needed no oxygen to carry. He extended his arm, which transformed smoothly into a drilling apparatus. 'These humans and their primitive rovers ... always searching in the wrong places. Too focused on the wrong things.'

He tapped a device attached to his wrist, examining the readings. 'Fifty meters below. Perfect.'

The drill engaged, cutting through the red rock with precision. As he worked, Eradax's exposed cranial exoskeleton—resembling a metal skull partially covered by a faceplate—tilted to examine the falling debris. His body featured rigid armour plates interlocked with flexible metal segments, allowing for fluid movement despite his imposing frame.

After several minutes, the ground beneath him gave way. Eradax controlled his descent using the thrusters built into his legs. The tunnel opened into a vast chamber that had not seen light for countless millennia.

'The Ancient outpost,' Eradax said with satisfaction, a hint of pleasure in his mechanical voice. 'Just as the archives suggested.'

The chamber was constructed of compressed Martian minerals, hardened to a material stronger than Earth's diamond. Strange symbols were etched into every surface. The architecture was distinctly non-human, with curved archways that defied conventional engineering.

Eradax moved with purpose towards the centre of the chamber where a pedestal stood. It was empty.

'Playing hard to get?' he asked the empty room, running his metallic fingers across the pedestal's surface. 'I do enjoy a challenge.'

He pressed down onto the middle of the pedestal. Yellow energy crackled from his fingertips, spreading across the ground in a web-like pattern. The symbols on the walls began to glow in response.

'Security systems still operational after forty thousand years,' he said, impressed. 'This will be more fun than I thought.'

The floor trembled, then split open. A hidden passage revealed itself, spiralling downward into darkness. Eradax descended without hesitation.

At the bottom, a second chamber awaited—smaller but more heavily fortified. In the centre, suspended in a field of pulsing energy, hovered a jagged crystalline object. It appeared to be made of an iridescent material that shifted colours as it rotated slowly in its containment field. Even from a distance, its power was palpable. The air around it seemed distorted, heavier.

The Gravity Shard.

Eradax took a step forward but stopped as a grinding noise echoed through the chamber. He wasn't alone.

'Guardian protocol activated,' announced a voice that seemed to come from the walls themselves. 'Identify yourself or be terminated.'

From an alcove emerged a figure nearly twice Eradax's size. It was formed from compressed Martian iron and stone, its surface the deep rust red of the planet's surface. Its face was crude but distinct, with hollow eyes that glowed with the same energy that surrounded the Shard.

'I am Eradax, Collector of Relics,' he replied, a hint of amusement in his tone. 'And you are in my way.'

The guardian responded by raising its arm. The air around Eradax suddenly compressed, pushing him to his knees as increased gravity pinned him down.

'Impressive,' Eradax said, struggling against the invisible force. 'The Ancients left a worthy protector. But I've faced far worse than you.'

With tremendous effort, he raised his hand. His fingers transformed, extending into blade-like appendages that glowed with yellow energy. He drove them into the floor, anchoring himself.

'Is that all you can do? Increase gravity?' he taunted, looking up at the guardian's face. 'Appropriate, yet disappointing.'

The guardian approached, each step causing the ground to crack under its weight. Eradax analysed the situation, calculating his next move while enjoying the momentary struggle.

As the guardian reached for him, he activated the weapons built into his exoskeleton. His chest plate opened, revealing an energy emitter that unleashed a shockwave of yellow power. The guardian staggered backwards, momentarily disrupted.

Eradax laughed, a cold mechanical sound. 'Let me show you how it's done.'

He lunged forward with impossible speed for something of his size, his right arm transforming into a blade that sliced through the guardian's shoulder. The wound revealed the interior composition of the being—layers of compressed minerals and ancient technology.

The guardian retaliated, smashing a fist into Eradax's side with enough force to send him crashing into the chamber wall. Impact warnings flashed across his vision.

'That,' Eradax said as he picked himself up, 'is going to cost you.'

He dodged the next attack, studying the guardian's movement patterns. Each attack was powerful but followed a predictable sequence. The guardian might be ancient technology, but it was still limited by its programming.

'You know what your problem is?' Eradax called out as he circled the massive figure. 'You lack creativity.'

He drew the guardian away from the pedestal. As it turned to follow, Eradax suddenly reversed direction, sliding between its legs. His hands transformed again, this time into claws that dug into the guardian's back.

'Your creators forgot one crucial detail,' he said as he climbed up the thrashing guardian, enjoying the creature's futile attempts to dislodge him. 'I've been hunting relics like yours for centuries. I learn. I adapt.'

Reaching the guardian's head, Eradax drove his now-weaponized hand directly into one of the glowing eyes. 'While you just follow orders.'

The guardian froze, then began to convulse as Eradax systematically destroyed its core systems.

'Don't worry,' Eradax whispered to it as its struggles weakened. 'Your relic will have a place of honour in my collection. That's more than most guardians can say for their treasures.'

The massive figure toppled forward, its light fading until it was nothing more than an inert sculpture of Martian stone. Eradax stood over it for a moment, savouring his victory before turning his attention back to the prize.

The Gravity Shard still hovered in its energy field, undisturbed by the battle. Eradax approached cautiously, examining the containment system.

'A quantum lock,' he determined. 'Very nice indeed. Let's see if I can outdo myself this time.'

He reached out with both hands, his fingers reconfiguring into complex tools as he worked to decipher the ancient security measures. After several minutes of careful manipulation, the energy field flickered and died.

The Shard dropped into his waiting palm.

The moment it touched him, Eradax felt its power—a sensation like holding a concentrated piece of a neutron star. The Shard was no larger than a helmet, its surface shifting with colours that shouldn't exist in the visible spectrum.

'Finally,' he said, studying his prize. 'After three centuries of searching.'

He opened a specialized containment unit on his belt, carefully placing the Shard inside. Unlike the other relics in his collection, this one would serve a greater purpose than mere display.

The chamber started to shake violently—the outpost's self-destruct sequence triggered by the removal of the Shard. Eradax made his way calmly towards the exit, untroubled by the collapse beginning around him.

'Always so dramatic, these ancient civilizations,' he remarked as chunks of ceiling crashed down around him. 'As if a little cave-in could stop me.'

Outside, his ship decloaked as he approached—a sleek vessel of the same metallic composition as its master. The boarding ramp extended, and Eradax entered without looking back at the plume of Martian dust rising from the collapsing outpost.

Inside the trophy chamber of his ship, Eradax placed the Gravity Shard in a specially designed display case. It joined dozens of other artefacts—each unique, each powerful, each representing a successful hunt.

'You'll do nicely,' he said to the Shard, watching as it pulsed with energy behind its containment field. 'When the time comes.'

He moved to the command centre of his vessel and reviewed the data on his next potential acquisition. The screen displayed a list of powerful artefacts scattered across the galaxy—each one meticulously researched, its location narrowed down through centuries of intelligence gathering.

'The Chronos Gauntlet can wait,' he decided, scrolling through the list. 'As can the Oracle Sphere and the Infinity Forge.'

His crimson eyes fixed on a particularly intriguing entry—a simple ring with unusual energy signatures—detected on a small blue planet in the solar system. Earth.

'Set course,' Eradax commanded his ship. 'I believe our next hunt will be ... entertaining.'

The ship's engines hummed to life as it broke orbit from Mars, accelerating towards deep space.

Chapter 1

The sun beamed over the grand courtyard of City, University of London and excited chatter filled the air. The momentous occasion had arrived – graduation day. Friends and family had gathered to celebrate the achievements of their loved ones, marking the culmination of years of dedication and hard work. Amid the sea of caps and gowns, one figure stood out: Simon Jones.

Clad in his graduation attire, Simon sat among his fellow graduands, his heart fluttering with a mixture of excitement and anticipation. The breeze rustled the fabric of his gown as he gazed ahead at the stage, where university officials and guest speakers were sharing words of wisdom. The realisation that he had successfully completed his studies in cybersecurity and was now about to receive his bachelor's degree was both thrilling and nerve-wracking.

Beside him sat Layla Thompson, the girl he had met at the university and who was now his girlfriend. Her eyes sparkled with enthusiasm as she leaned playfully against his shoulder. Her presence offered him a sense of calm within the throng of students and amid the grandeur of the occasion. His lips curved into a soft smile as he pulled her close.

The speeches continued, a blend of inspiration and encouragement that echoed within the courtyard. Simon absorbed every word, his thoughts drifting between the words spoken and the journey that had led him to this moment: his late-night study sessions, the camaraderie of his classmates and the countless hours dedicated to mastering the intricacies of cybersecurity.

Then the time finally arrived for the graduands to be called up individually. Simon's heart raced as his name came through the speakers, prompting a sense of accomplishment to swell within him. With steady steps, he made his way onto the stage, his stride reflecting the resilience that had carried him through his academic journey.

The moment he received his degree certificate etched itself into his memory. The applause of his fellow students and the cheering from the audience swamped him in a wave of celebration. He looked out into the blur of faces, his eyes locking onto the familiar ones that held unwavering support for him: his mother, Sarah, and his younger sister, Tessa. Their smiles radiated pride, filling Simon with a sense of gratitude. Above the applause, Layla's cheers resonated in the air. Her clapping hands and beaming smile mirrored his own joy and for a moment their eyes locked, reaffirming their shared connection.

As the ceremony drew to a close, Simon and his fellow graduates left their seats to rejoin their families and the courtyard buzzed with a vibrant energy and shared laughter. Filled with anticipation, Simon scanned the crowd for his mother and sister. Finally spotting them, he rushed over, a grin spreading across his face.

'Mum! Tessa!' he exclaimed, his voice laced with excitement.

Sarah's arms enveloped him, her pride evident in the way she held him close, while Tessa clung to him, her enthusiasm matched only by her affection for her older brother.

Within the embrace, Simon's voice softened, a note of nostalgia tingeing his words. 'Wish Dad could've been here,' he said, his tone full of melancholy.

Sarah gently pulled back and looked at her son, a shared understanding passing between them. 'He would've been so proud of you. Both your father and James,' she replied, her voice soft and reassuring.

For Simon, they were the two people with whom he wished he could have shared this euphoric moment of his life.

His pensive moment was interrupted by Layla's arrival, her smile radiant as she approached them. 'Congratulations, Simon!' she exclaimed, her voice a joyful melody.

Simon smiled at the sight of his girlfriend and pulled her in for a side hug. 'You and I both.'

'Mrs Jones, Tessa, it's a pleasure to see you both again,' Layla said, turning to hug them.

'Likewise, Layla. It's always wonderful to have you around,' Sarah said, gently squeezing Layla's hand.

Layla's laughter tinkled through the air. 'Thank you. You've been more than welcoming, and I really appreciate it.'

Sarah gestured towards her son, her eyes twinkling. 'Well, he did say you were the reason he survived his programming classes.'

Layla's eyes danced with amusement. 'I'll take that as a compliment.'

Sarah's expression softened as she regarded the two young adults before her. 'Let's continue the celebrations this evening at a restaurant. You're both invited.'

Simon's face lit up at the prospect of continuing the celebration. 'Absolutely, Mum! We'll be there.'

Sarah exchanged a knowing smile with Simon and gave him a playful nudge. 'You go on, have fun. We'll catch up with you later.'

Simon blushed as he glanced at Layla and then his mum and sister. 'All right, Mum. See you there.'

With a final wave, Simon and Layla headed off, their laughter mingling with the joyous ambiance of the day. The graduation ceremony was now in the rearview, and a new chapter of their lives would begin, one that Simon was eager to explore.

Chapter 2

The automatic chime of the convenience store door announced Simon's arrival, its cheerful jingle ringing throughout the shop. Inside the brightly lit store, the scent of packaged snacks and fresh newspapers greeted him. Running his hand over his short hair, he patted the raindrops from his head as he moved past the aisles of neatly stacked merchandise. He made his way over to the beverage fridge and eyed the soft drinks, looking for the flavour he desired. Settling on orange, he scooped it up, then considered which one he should get for Layla.

As he reached back into the fridge, the door chime announced another customer. Turning to look over his shoulder, Simon was struck by the strange appearance of the man who had just walked into the store. He wore a black balaclava, and one of his hands was concealed inside his long blue jacket. Following behind him was another man, who was wearing a red balaclava, his hand deep within one of his pockets. With his back to the door, the second man brandished a large knife, holding it low, just below his waist.

Alarm bells went off in Simon's head and the atmosphere suddenly became charged. Something bad was about to go down. Instinctively, he touched his silver Ring, but before he could make a move, he felt cold metal press against the nape of his neck.

'Don't you even twitch, fam,' commanded a feminine but menacing voice.

Simon quickly surmised the situation. A robbery was about to take place, and he was being held hostage. Even for a city like London, armed crime like this was excessive. Whether or not the thieves had murderous intent, he didn't know, but he wasn't keen on waiting to find out. He glanced over to the front of the store where the shop assistant was standing terrified behind the till. The man in the black balaclava pointed his pistol at the middle-aged man and threw a bag onto the counter.

'Yo, empty the till into the bag, blud! Patterned quick, yeah?' barked the thief, gesturing aggressively.

The assistant, with shaking hands, complied with the thief's demands, grasping at the money in the till and stuffing it into the bag.

'Try anything stupid and my mandem will chef you up proper,' warned the thief in the black balaclava, glancing at his accomplice near the door. The man in the red balaclava raised his knife aggressively as if to demonstrate he would make good on the threat.

The situation was escalating quickly. Simon knew he had to act now. He hadn't intended to use his powers this early, but duty called. His mind shifted gear as he analysed the situation: three thugs, two with guns and one with a large knife. Making subtle movements with his head, he glanced up at the corners of the room and the ceiling. He appeared to be in a blind spot. Perfect. He could stop the crime while maintaining his anonymity.

'Move again and I'll put one in your head, get me?' said the voice behind him, pressing the cold metal harder against his neck.

Hearing this, Simon prepped himself for the decision he was about to make.

You ready? The voice of the Fallen Ring echoed in his head.

Simon took a deep breath. *Yeah. But we don't transform. On my count: three, two, one …*

As soon as he reached one, Simon spun around and clotheslined the woman who was holding the gun to his head, knocking her unconscious before she hit the floor. Before turning back towards the others, he pulled his grey hood low over his face to protect his anonymity. As he turned to face the front of the store, the man in the black balaclava shouted to his lackey by the door who looked up and launched himself down the aisle towards Simon, his knife clutched in his hand.

'Shank this wasteman!' the leader yelled.

Closing the distance, the thug lunged at Simon, aiming for his stomach, but Simon was much faster than he had anticipated. Dodging the blade, Simon kicked the man's shin, bringing him down to one knee, before hammering his fist into his face, sending the thug crashing headfirst onto the shop floor.

With two down and one to go, Simon turned his attention to the man in the black balaclava, who ran towards him, his pistol aimed at Simon's chest.

'You're dead, bruv! Dead!' he shouted frantically.

But just as he pulled the trigger, Simon's armoured hand shot out and covered the muzzle, quieting the sound of the gunshot and containing the impact. The thief stopped in his tracks, his eyes widening as he looked at Simon's hand in disbelief. Seizing the moment, Simon rammed his fist into the man's stomach, before lifting him up and hurling him into the shelves, rendering the thug motionless.

With the situation diffused, Simon vitiated the criminals' guns by stomping on their barrels and then ran out of the store, past the shop assistant whose mouth was hanging open. He had no desire to draw unnecessary attention to himself, nor could he risk revealing his identity. If his cover was blown, he was certain there would be enough criminals looking for revenge, which was a dangerous can of worms.

The soft drinks would have to wait for the time being.

Chapter 3

The city's heartbeat pulsed beneath the velvety blanket of the night sky. A million lights shimmered across the sprawling canvas of London, casting an ethereal glow that painted the urban landscape with a sense of wonder. Above the towering structures and bustling streets, Simon was sitting on a rooftop ledge, his legs dangling over the precipice, looking down on the panorama that lay before him. He found solace in this lofty vantage point. The city's nocturnal soundscape, a blend of distant sirens and muffled conversations, served as a backdrop to his thoughts. The wind whispered secrets in his ears, its gentle caress a reminder of the freedom that came with the darkened skies.

His eyes traced the contours of the London skyline, and his mind drifted back to earlier in the day – his graduation ceremony, which had marked the end of one chapter and the beginning of another. The memory of Layla's radiant smile and the applause of his loved ones reverberated in his thoughts. He was older now, a young man whose future was brimming with possibilities. He would soon be starting his new role at a prominent cybersecurity firm. His dedication had paid off, securing him a full-time position after acing the interview. But this was more than a job, it was the first steppingstone in his career, and he would soon leave behind the part-time administrative position that had sustained him during his university years.

He looked down at his hand where the silver Ring gleamed. A gift from the universe, it had granted him abilities that transcended the realm of ordinary existence. A whisper echoed in his mind – the voice of the Ring: *You are no longer the teenager who stumbled upon us.* The resonance of the voice was both enigmatic and comforting. *You have become the bearer of our shared legacy and the Guardian of its potential.*

He traced the outline of the Ring as he contemplated the truth of its words. The journey that had led him to this rooftop, to this crossroads of identity, was a testament to his evolution. The Ring had unlocked doors to immense power as well as great responsibility, and he had embraced it as best as he could.

Using the Ring's power, he donned his dark-purple alter ego, becoming the silent protector of London's night-time. The transformation was more than physical; it was a shift in identity, an acknowledgement of the dual nature that defined his existence. His alter ego was more than a disguise; it was a reflection of the latent strength within him.

A thrill coursed through his veins as he rose to his feet, his body moving with a grace that belied his other identity. The winds that danced around him seemed to respond to his newfound confidence, as if acknowledging the synergy between his alter ego and the pulse of the city.

With each leap and bound, he revelled in the exhilaration of the night. He scaled walls, leaped across rooftops and defied gravity with a fluidity that was second nature to him now. The city was his playground, a canvas upon which he could etch his signature. The thrill of movement, the rush of wind against his face – it was an expression of freedom experienced by only a select few. Yet despite the rush, his thoughts remained tethered to the responsibilities that accompanied his alter ego. The Fallen Ring had granted him extraordinary abilities, but its power was not to be taken lightly. It was a force that could alter realities, a tool for betterment, or a weapon of mass destruction. Its temptation could easily sway even the noblest of hearts.

The voice of the Ring echoed once more in his mind, its presence a constant reminder of the choices he must make: *You've demonstrated that your path is not one of power alone. Balance must be your watchword, for it is easy to tip either way.*

Simon perched on the edge of a rooftop, his eyes closed for a brief moment, his thoughts aligned with the weight of his calling. He wasn't just a young man with ambition; he was a Guardian, a protector, a beacon of hope in a world often shadowed by deadly sins.

An intangible tingling vibrating through the air drew him from his thoughts. The Ring's voice grew clearer, its tone alert: *It's time to return to work, Simon.*

Opening his eyes, Simon's resolve solidified. He leaped from the rooftop, his body descending gracefully through the night, a shadow in pursuit of justice. The robbery attempt at the convenience store had merely been the beginning of the crimes he would stop tonight.

CHAPTER 4

T he night hung heavy over the city, cloaking its alleys and hidden corners in a shroud of darkness. Among those who thrived in the shadows was a criminal gang of four men. Travelling through the city streets in a black Jeep, they were focused on their next job. In the passenger seat was Wei Zhang, the skilled technician of the group whose nimble fingers had cracked more safes than he could count. In the rear seats sat Callum Briggs, the rookie whose nervous energy was palpable, next to Mateo Reyes, the brawn of the group whose hulking frame barely fit in the vehicle. In the driver's seat was Dushane Barracks, the brains of the group and the man who called the shots. Tonight, he was leading his team to an orphanage for a robbery. The word on the street was that the underfunded charity had recently come into a massive cash windfall thanks to an anonymous donation – over half a million pounds, or so the whispers went. For Dushane's crew of career criminals, it was the perfect opportunity – too enticing to pass up.

The Jeep slowed to a crawl as Dushane surveyed the area around the old orphanage building. Tucked away on a quiet side street, it seemed deserted for the night. Killing the headlights, he coasted to a stop in a back alley around the corner.

'All right, listen up,' he growled, turning to face his men. 'Wei, Mateo, you're with me. Callum, you're on lookout duty in the car.'

Callum's eyes widened in the rearview mirror. 'What? Why do I have to stay behind?'

Dushane fixed the younger man with a withering look. 'In case the Guardian shows up. We can't risk dead weight slowing us down if he gets involved.'

A nervous chuckle escaped Callum's lips. 'The Guardian? That's just a myth, Boss. I didn't think—'

'I've seen him,' Dushane said flatly, his tone dead serious, 'with my own eyes. He ain't no joke. And if he gets wind of this job, I'm damn near certain he'll try to stop us. So, you're staying in the car and keeping watch. Understand?'

Callum opened his mouth as if to protest further, but simply gave a small nod.

Dushane turned his attention to the others. 'Mask up, grab the kit and duffel bags. We get in, get the money, get out. No mistakes. No distractions. This is a straightforward smash-and-grab, nothing more.'

They pulled on black ski masks, further obscuring their features in the darkness, and placed tools and supplies in a small black bag: Wei's lock picks and small, shaped charges to blow the safe's hinges if needed. Mateo, however, didn't need any tools. He strapped on an exoskeleton suit – a matte-black armoured frame that encased his arms and upper body. Servomotors whirred as the mechanical muscles activated, augmenting Mateo's already impressive strength.

Moving quickly and quietly, the three men made their way through the inky shadows towards the rear entrance of the orphanage. The thick metal door looked imposing, but it posed little difficulty for Mateo in his exoskeleton suit. Grunting with effort, he heaved against the door's handle with one armoured hand, his other pushing against the frame. Hydraulics hissed as the suit's servo-powered arms engaged. Slowly, but inexorably, the heavy door began to bend outwards, its frame warping and bolts popping loose from the brickwork. With one final heave, Mateo ripped it open, the shriek of tortured metal filling the still night air.

'Madre de Dios,' Mateo whispered with a grin, flexing the mechanical arms. 'I could get used to this power.'

The trio slipped inside, their senses on high alert, and wound through a maze of dimly lit hallways, Wei leading the way with Dushane and Mateo close behind. The orphanage seemed deserted, not a sound save for their muffled footfall. Eventually, they came upon the small records office where the safe was kept.

Wei made quick work of the outer door, his nimble fingers working the tumblers until the lock clicked open. Behind the door was a heavy cast-iron safe, its surface smooth and featureless. From the black bag, he pulled out a stethoscope and small drill bit. Pressing the scope against the frame of the safe, he began to drill into the casing to locate the lock mechanism.

'Precision over power,' Wei murmured to himself in Mandarin, his focus absolute.

While he worked, Dushane and Mateo kept watch, their eyes roving constantly for any sign of movement. Mateo's exoskeleton whined softly as servos autonomically adjusted to keep him balanced and ready to spring into action. Several tense minutes ticked by before they heard a muffled clunk from within the safe.

Wei grinned beneath his mask. 'Got it,' he murmured, carefully turning the final tumbler.

The heavy door of the safe swung open with a groan to reveal their hard-won prize: stacks upon stacks of neatly bundled banknotes. Mateo let out a low whistle as he pulled the duffel bags off his shoulder. He wasted no time shovelling the cash inside, wads of bills disappearing by the fistful.

As Mateo worked, Wei turned to Dushane. 'Tell me again, Boss, you ever think about what we're doing here? Hitting an orphanage for cash—'

'No!' said Dushane, his eyes cold and unfeeling. He shook his head curtly. 'No. We do what we have to do. Take what we can, when we can, however we can. Having second thoughts? That's weakness. And weakness breeds fear. Fear gets in the way of opportunity. That's why we don't tolerate weakness, not in this life. At the end of the day, it's a job and this is our payment.'

Wei was silent for a moment, watching as Mateo transferred the remaining money. 'Yeah ... I guess you're right.' He sighed. 'Opportunities like this don't come along too often.'

Grabbing and bagging the last wodge of cash, Mateo froze as an alarm tore through the silence of the room. He looked up, panic filling his eyes.

'Must have been a failsafe tied to the safe's weight,' said Dushane, his voice a low growl. 'Grab the bags. We need to move. Now!'

They scarpered back through the corridors towards the exit, the high-pitched alarm ringing in their ears and the duffel bags weighing them down.

Outside, the engine of the Jeep roared into life, headlights blazing as Callum waited anxiously behind the wheel. Dushane's heart pounded in his chest as he flung open the boot and they began tossing in the heavy bags of cash. A sense of impending danger was thick in the air, the tension reaching its zenith when Dushane eyed something materialising from the shadows. Like a spectre it emerged, forming a humanoid shape.

'Stealing from an orphanage ... now that's an all-time low, fellas,' said the looming figure, its words laced with a chilling certainty.

Dushane's breath caught in his throat as cold realisation washed over him. The Guardian, the mythical being that safeguarded the city. He was standing before them, fixing them with his bright-purple eyes.

'N-not you ... n-not now ...' Dushane stammered, unable to tear his eyes away.

Wei recovered first, whipping out his snub-nosed revolver and firing a flurry of rounds as the figure approached. But the bullets were merely absorbed and discarded by the Guardian as he continued to advance undeterred. With a savage grunt, Mateo charged the vigilante head on, his exoskeleton suit augmenting his forward momentum into a battering ram of fury. But before Mateo could make contact, the Guardian front flipped over him, then turned one of its hands into a tendril-like appendage and smacked the gun out of Wei's hand. Wei recoiled and the purple vigilante rushed forward and slammed him into a brick wall.

Dushane, rooted to the spot, watched the events unfold as if his mind was struggling to process the supernatural scene playing out before him. But as Wei slumped unconscious to the ground and Mateo attempted to hold off the humanoid, his survival instincts finally kicked in. Spinning on his heel, he sprinted for the Jeep, throwing himself into the passenger seat.

'Get us out of here, now!' he screamed at Callum, who seemed paralysed behind the wheel, his eyes wide with terror.

Callum's hands shook violently on the gearshift, his feet working the pedals in a frenzy, desperately trying to find the biting point of the clutch. After several white-knuckled seconds, the transmission finally engaged with a grinding of gears, and the Jeep shot forward, its tyres screeching against the asphalt, putting distance between them and the crime scene.

Dushane turned in his seat and glanced out the window. Mateo swung a haymaker with his exoskeleton only for the Guardian to catch his arm and twist it before kicking him to the midsection, sending him off his feet and into the wall. Sparks flew from Mateo's exoskeleton and he collapsed to the ground in a heap.

'We can't just leave them!' Callum shouted, his voice cracking with panic as the Jeep bucked beneath them.

'Just drive!' Dushane snarled, his fists tightly clenched. 'Get us out of here!'

Through the rear window, Dushane caught sight of the Guardian. Those incandescent purple eyes burning in the night, fixed upon them with an unyielding intensity. A chill shot down his spine as hatred welled up inside him. If they managed to escape tonight, this wouldn't be the end—it would be just the beginning.

The look in those glowing eyes was unmistakable. The Guardian wasn't about to let them go unpunished.

CHAPTER 5

Adrenaline pulsed through Simon's body as he stood among the shadows, his alter ego exuding an air of vowed vengeance, his eyes narrowing on the tail lights of the black Jeep. He had subdued and tied up two of the robbers with some loose metal chains, but there was no time for respite. Two criminals were fleeing, their attempt at escape further fuelling his resolve to bring them to justice.

Those bastards won't get far, the Fallen Ring whispered in his mind. *They really thought they could rob an orphanage and just drive away?*

Simon's lips tightened. 'Not in my city,' he murmured, his voice barely audible even to himself.

With a bound, he leaped onto the ledge of a nearby building, his body merging seamlessly with the night as he took off in pursuit. The world around him transformed into a blur of motion – a blend of streetlights, billboards and buildings that whizzed by in a breathtaking display of agility. His heart raced as he bounded from rooftop to rooftop, the thrill of the chase coursing through his veins. He was a force of nature, a phantom that hunted criminals.

Ahead of him, the Jeep darted through the streets, carving a desperate and dangerous path between the lanes. But Simon matched its speed, his agile movements allowing him to keep pace as the car weaved through the alleys and avenues of London. These criminals appeared to be a cut above the common ones, but he was confident he could catch them. The Jeep raced on, but his mind remained one step ahead, calculating its course, anticipating the next move. With a final burst of speed, he soared from a rooftop, his body tracing an arc through the air before he landed gracefully on the roof of a nearby building. The Jeep hurtled around a corner, its tyres screeching against the pavement as it barrelled down a narrow street. Simon's lips curled into a determined grin. He knew their course, and there would be no escape.

The night air whipped against his form as he took off once more, his feet barely skimming the rooftops as he propelled himself forward. The glow of the streetlamps cast long shadows that seemed to dance in rhythm with his movements. His breathing was steady and his focus unbroken as he maintained the chase.

They're heading towards Whitechapel, the Ring observed. *Trying to lose us in the maze of side streets.*

'Not happening,' Simon replied, his eyes tracking the Jeep's erratic movements through the thinning traffic of the late-night roads.

Suddenly, his acute senses caught a glimpse of a couple stepping onto a pedestrian crossing, unaware of the impending danger. The Jeep was hurtling towards them, its speed leaving them vulnerable to a collision that would prove catastrophic. Changing course, he surged towards the crossing, his muscles propelling him towards the vulnerable couple. Reaching them in an instant, he wrapped his arms around them and swept them out of harm's way. The screeching tyres and thunderous roar of the Jeep's engine were silenced by Simon's intervention, the world reduced to a tableau of suspended time.

The couple, their hearts racing, looked up at the figure who had saved them. Simon's dark silhouette was a paradox – equal parts guardian and enigma. They exchanged a bewildered look, their eyes a mixture of shock and gratitude.

'You're safe now,' Simon said, his voice a reassuring whisper. And then, as abruptly as he had intervened, he set them back on the pavement, his focus shifting back to the unfinished pursuit of the Jeep that continued its reckless flight, weaving its path through blurred streets and sharp turns.

Two lives saved, the Ring noted with approval. *But those criminals nearly killed innocent people. Time to end this chase.*

Simon was relentless now, his pursuit fuelled by the need to put an end to the criminals' desperate escape. They had already endangered a few lives; he wouldn't let them endanger any more. The distance between Simon and the fleeing Jeep began to close as the black vehicle weaved through the arteries of the city, its headlights piercing the darkness in twin beams of defiance. Simon's breath quickened; he was getting closer, his prey almost within reach.

With one final burst of speed, he leaped from the ledge of a building, barrelling through the air in a calculated trajectory and landing on the roof of the Jeep, the impact barely causing a ripple in his fluid motions. From his vantage point, he bent down and peered through the windscreen, his eyes blazing with a mix of anger and excitement. Inside the vehicle, the criminals were wide-eyed with fear, their eyes locked on the fearsome figure that had materialised before them once again. Callum's hands trembled on the wheel and, for a moment, he lost control as the Jeep veered dangerously close to the edge of disaster, the wheels grazing the high kerb, the sudden impact jolting the vehicle. The criminals' hearts raced, their instincts screaming as Callum struggled to regain control. But it was too late. The car flipped over, the world spinning in a chaotic whirlwind.

Simon's instincts kicked in as the Jeep rolled, his body moving with a grace that defied the laws of physics. He lunged forward, his arms extending to catch the vehicle just above the pavement, the sheer strength of his alter ego bearing the considerable weight. Holding the car aloft, he planted his feet, his muscles taut as he stabilised the vehicle above him. With a powerful thrust, he righted the car in a fluid and controlled motion. The Jeep landed on its four wheels with a muted thud, its momentum completely halted.

Inside the car, Dushane and Callum slumped in dazed silence, their senses reeling from the violent upheaval. In the passenger seat, Dushane cowered before the Guardian's intimidating form.

There was nowhere to run now.

Simon reached through the cracked driver's window, seizing Callum by the collar and lifting him effortlessly from his seat. The young criminal dangled in his grip, eyes wide with terror.

'P-please,' Callum stammered, his voice cracking. 'I was just the driver—it wasn't my idea!'

'Save it for the police,' Simon growled, his voice deliberately deepened to conceal his identity. 'You chose to be part of this.'

Callum's legs kicked uselessly in the air. 'Who ... who are you?'

Simon paused, his glowing eyes narrowing as he considered the question. 'I'm the Guardian,' he replied, the name feeling right as it left his lips. 'And I'm watching over this city.'

The impasse was shattered by the sound of approaching police sirens, their wailing chorus drawing nearer with each passing moment. Simon glanced towards the flashing blue lights in the distance. It was time to leave. Reaching inside the vehicle, he restrained the criminals within their seats, his actions precise and efficient. He met their panicked gazes with a stern warning: 'These streets are protected. Remember that when you're sitting in your cells.'

As the sirens grew louder, the Guardian cast a final glance at the criminals, his eyes vigilant and judging, before he merged with the shadows, his figure fading into the obscurity of the night once more. It had been another successful night of stopping crime. The pursuit had ended, but it was only a taste of what was to come.

That was impressive, the Ring commented as Simon scaled a nearby building, seeking higher ground to observe the arrival of the police. *You're getting better at this.*

Simon crouched on the rooftop edge, watching as police vehicles surrounded the Jeep. Officers approached with caution, weapons drawn as they discovered the restrained criminals.

'They robbed an orphanage,' Simon said quietly, disgust evident in his tone. 'Who does that?'

Desperate people. Ruthless people, the Ring replied. *The kind this city could do less of.*

Simon nodded, his eyes tracking the officers as they pulled Dushane from the passenger seat. Even from this distance, he could see the fury in the man's eyes as he was handcuffed and led to a police car. There was something unsettling about the way Dushane scanned the rooftops, as if searching for the Guardian's silhouette against the night sky.

He's looking for you, the Ring observed.

'Let him look,' Simon replied, rising to his feet as the police secured the scene. 'He won't find me.'

But as Dushane was pushed into the back of the police car, his gaze seemed to lock directly onto Simon's position. A chill ran down Simon's spine as he saw the hatred burning in those eyes—a silent but seething promise of retribution.

He'll remember you, the Ring warned. They all will.

Simon turned away, his form melting into the shadows once more. 'Good,' he said firmly. 'Then maybe they'll think twice before they try something like this again.'

As he made his way across the London skyline, heading home after a night's work, Simon couldn't shake the feeling that this wasn't the end of his encounter with this particular set of criminals. Especially the older guy in the passenger seat. His energy was dark. This wasn't the last Simon would see of him.

But for tonight, at least, he had won. The orphanage's money would be returned, and four criminals were on their way to face justice. Not bad for an evening's work.

Layla's still waiting for that orange soda, the Ring reminded him with a hint of amusement.

Simon smiled as he disappeared into the night. Some things would have to wait until tomorrow.

***

The police car's interior felt suffocating. Dushane sat rigid against the hard plastic seat, his wrists raw against the cold metal of the handcuffs. Outside, blue lights painted the London streets in rhythmic flashes as they drove towards the station. But Dushane saw none of it. His mind was elsewhere—replaying the night's events on an endless, torturous loop.

They had never failed before. Not like this. His crew had built a reputation on precision, on success. From bank vaults to high-end jewellery stores, they had always walked away with the prize. Until tonight. Until him.

The Guardian.

Dushane's jaw clenched so tight he could feel his teeth might crack. The humiliation burned worse than any physical pain—being plucked from the sky like a helpless child, watching his carefully assembled team scattered and captured. Half a million pounds, gone. Freedom, gone. Respect, gone.

All because of some freak in a costume, or whatever that thing was.

Through the wire mesh dividing the car, Dushane could hear the officers chattering excitedly about the Guardian's latest exploit. London's mysterious protector. The city's shadowy saviour. Each word was like a knife twisting in his gut.

'They say he's not even human,' one officer remarked. 'Did you see what he did to the car? Caught it mid-flip like it was nothing.'

Dushane's hands balled into fists, the handcuffs biting deeper into his flesh. He barely felt it. The rage coursing through him was too consuming, too pure to leave room for something as trivial as pain.

This wasn't over. It couldn't be. Prison walls wouldn't hold him forever—couldn't hold any of them forever. Wei, Mateo, Callum—they were survivors, like him. And when they got out, they'd be stronger. Smarter. Ready.

As the police car turned a corner, Dushane stared up at the London skyline, scanning the rooftops where the Guardian had vanished. A vow crystallized in his mind, hardening like steel.

'I'm coming for you,' he whispered, his breath fogging the window. 'Whatever it takes, however long it takes. I will find you. And when I do ...'

He let the thought hang unfinished in the darkness. Some promises were too profound, too visceral for words. But in the silence of the police car, as London slipped by outside, Dushane Barracks made a covenant with vengeance itself.

The Guardian would fall. And Dushane would be the one to bring him down.

CHAPTER 6

The sleek vessel cut through Earth's atmosphere, its hull made of the same strange metallic alloy as its master, absorbing rather than reflecting the moonlight. Inside the command centre, Eradax stood motionless, his angular metallic form silhouetted against the glow of multiple screens displaying information about this primitive world. His crimson eyes narrowed as he surveyed the readouts.

'Atmosphere analysis complete,' announced the ship's AI in a monotone voice. 'Composition suitable for sustained presence. No immediate biological hazards detected.'

Eradax's fingers—long, articulated metal digits—tapped against the control panel. 'Maintain stealth protocols. These primitives possess rudimentary detection systems, but I will not risk exposure. Not yet.'

The vessel descended silently through cloud cover, its advanced propulsion system leaving no heat signature for Earth's monitoring stations to detect. Eradax had chosen his landing site carefully. The geometric structures below—three distinct pyramidal forms rising from the desert floor—had intrigued him during his preliminary scans. Ancient constructions, built by hand if the ship's historical analysis was accurate. Perhaps primitive, but not without a certain ... elegance.

'Landing sequence initiated,' the AI reported as the ship settled into the shadow of a rocky outcrop, several kilometres from the nearest human settlement.

The moment the landing mechanism engaged, Eradax felt it—a pulse, distant but unmistakable. A ring unlike any other. The Fallen Ring. Its energy signature called to him across continents, a siren song of power that had drawn him across the void between stars.

'So,' he murmured, his voice a metallic rasp. 'It is actually here.'

The main hatch hissed open, and Eradax stepped onto Earth for the first time. The dry desert air met his sensory receptors, carrying molecules of sand, stone, and the distant scent of the human civilization nearby. He stood motionless, acclimating, analysing.

This was not the first world he had visited in his relentless pursuit of artefacts, but something about this planet felt different. It hummed with potential, with life, with a chaotic energy unlike the sterile, regulated environments of his long-destroyed homeworld.

Eradax moved across the sand with surprising grace for his imposing form. The Great Pyramid loomed before him, its limestone facing eroded by millennia of wind and sand, yet still magnificent in the moonlight.

'Primitive construction,' he observed aloud. 'Yet they stand after thousands of their years. Perhaps these humans possess more ingenuity than my initial assessment suggested.'

His crimson gaze swept across the structure, sensors penetrating its stone mass, mapping internal chambers and corridors. Nothing of value to him here—no artefacts of power, no technologies beyond simple mechanical traps and chambers. Yet the builders had achieved something that impressed even him: endurance. These monuments had outlasted their creators, their civilization, perhaps even their purpose.

On his homeworld, nothing so primitive would have been permitted to exist. Inefficiency had been eliminated, progress constantly accelerating until the inevitable collapse. Before the end, their cities had been marvels of crystalline towers and quantum architecture, structures that shifted and adapted to environmental conditions. All gone now, reduced to particulate matter scattered across their star system.

A sound caught his attention—human voices, approaching. Tourists, most likely, coming to view the monuments by moonlight. Eradax activated his cloaking field, rendering himself invisible to their limited visual spectrum.

They passed within meters of where he stood—a family, two adults and a child, speaking excitedly in one of the planet's countless languages. His translation system processed their words automatically: expressions of wonder, historical facts, mundane conversation.

So fragile. So unaware of what moved among them.

The child stopped suddenly, looking directly towards where Eradax stood concealed. For a moment, he wondered if his cloaking had malfunctioned. But then the child simply pointed at the pyramid behind him, chattering about its height.

Eradax's metallic lips curled into what might have been a smile. 'Curious creatures,' he whispered, too low for human ears. 'You sense something beyond your understanding, yet lack the capacity to recognise it.'

He could have reached out, could have taken one of them for study. It would have been simple—his strength far exceeded theirs, and his ship contained analysis chambers that could extract every secret from their fragile biology. But such actions would draw attention. The time for that would come, but not yet. Not until he had secured his prize.

Returning to his vessel, Eradax reviewed the planetary scans. Earth's technology was advancing rapidly, but remained millennia behind what his homeworld had achieved before its fall. Rudimentary space exploration, increasingly complex computer systems, primitive artificial intelligence. They had only just begun harnessing nuclear energy in any meaningful way.

Yet there was something almost ... admirable in their determination. Despite their short lifespans and limited resources, these humans strove constantly upward. In some ways, they reminded him of his own species, before ambition had led to destruction.

'Display energy signature tracking,' he commanded.

The holographic display shifted, revealing a pulsing point of light thousands of kilometres distant. London, according to the geographic database his ship had extracted from Earth's information networks. The Fallen Ring's energy was unmistakable, even at this distance—a reality-affecting power that called to him like nothing else in his vast collection.

'How strange,' Eradax mused, studying the readings more closely. 'The signature fluctuates. It appears the Ring has bonded with a host.' His crimson eyes narrowed. 'This complicates matters.'

In all his centuries of collecting, he had pursued rumours of Fallen Rings many times, but never succeeded in acquiring one. The prospect of finding an active Ring, one that had chosen a living host ... that presented both challenges and opportunities unlike anything in his vast collection.

The ship's computer chimed softly. 'Warning: local communication satellites changing orbit. Possible detection risk in current position.'

Eradax straightened. 'Prepare for relocation. Set course for optimal observation distance from the Ring's location.'

As the ship hummed to life around him, Eradax reviewed what he knew of Fallen Rings. Relics of immense power, forged by one of the Superlunary Ones—entities that existed beyond the mortal realm. Each Ring was crafted with subtle distinctions, imbued with timeless wisdom and extraordinary power. They were sentient in their own way, capable of bonding with compatible hosts, granting abilities that defied conventional physics.

Despite all his centuries of collecting, a Fallen Ring had always eluded him. The rarity of these artefacts was matched only by their potency. The excitement of finally acquiring one sent a charge through his circuits—this could be the crowning jewel of his collection.

'I have crossed galaxies for lesser prizes,' he said to himself as the ship rose silently into the night. 'Whatever host you have chosen, whatever protection you believe you have found ... it is temporary.'

The vessel accelerated, banking northward towards Europe, leaving no trace of its presence save for a single set of inhuman footprints in the desert sand—prints that the wind would erase before dawn.

'All artefacts return to the Collector, in time.'

CHAPTER 7

The early morning sun cast a golden hue over the city's skyline, sweeping the metropolis in an amber light that signalled the start of a new day and the shedding of an old one. As brightness poured through the parting clouds, the cityscape was bathed in a beautiful blend of pale orange and soft lavender that was reflected in the towering skyscrapers that stretched towards the heavens, as if in an effort to bask in the natural brilliance.

On top of a skyscraper, Simon Jones stood in quiet solitude and contemplation, the events of the previous night still in his mind. He rolled his shoulders, feeling the lingering soreness from the confrontation at the orphanage. The criminals' capture had cost him in bruises and strained muscles—a physical reminder of the price of his chosen path. Yet, as always, the Fallen Ring had accelerated his healing, the worst of his injuries already fading to memory.

It had been a successful intervention, one that had thwarted the criminal gang's heist at the orphanage, followed by a harrowing chase that had saved innocent lives from their speeding getaway car. He had prevailed in his duty as a protector once again. And yet, as the sun's rays illuminated the horizon, a question gnawed at his consciousness: could he continue down this path indefinitely? The question hung in the air like a shroud, tugging at Simon's thoughts as he gazed out over the sprawling cityscape. He had become accustomed to his role as London's silent guardian, putting a dent in its crime and corruption. But beneath the veneer of strength lay a niggling uncertainty, an uncertainty he couldn't shake.

As his mind wrestled with the weight of his identity, the voice of the Fallen Ring emerged in his thoughts. *How will you answer this question, Simon?* Its cadence carried counsel and invited contemplation.

Simon's brows furrowed as he engaged in the internal dialogue, his mind seeking clarity among the complex emotions that churned within him. The Ring's presence had been a constant companion, offering advice and much invaluable insight. And yet, as he contemplated his future, he wondered whether he could truly lay down the mantle of the vigilante he had become.

Taking a break, even temporarily, might be wise, the Ring's voice continued, its tone a mixture of encouragement and reflection. *You have given much to this city, Simon. Your journey towards redemption has been marked by your actions, and perhaps it is right to spend some time away to deeply reflect—on what it is you want.*

Simon continued to stare down upon the city below, its streets a blur of constant movement.

A life less burdened, a life in which he could share his days with Layla without the constant tug of the duties of his alter ego was an attractive proposition. It was a concept that held both allure and anxiety – a crossroads where his identity as a protector and his desire for a normal existence converged.

Simon thought back to their dinner last week, how Layla had looked at him with concern when he'd made an excuse to leave early after hearing police sirens. '"You always disappear when something's happening in the city,"' she'd said, her fingers lightly touching his hand across the table. '"Sometimes I wonder if you're running towards trouble instead of away from it."' Her intuition had cut closer to the truth than she knew. He couldn't keep lying to those perceptive eyes.

'But could I truly step away?' Simon's thoughts spilled forth as he voiced his inner conflict. 'Could I leave behind this life, even with all its thrills, challenges and sacrifices?'

The Ring's voice resonated in his mind. *The path you choose is yours, Simon. I offer counsel, but the decisions that shape your destiny rest within you. We've been together long enough for me to trust your judgement.*

Simon mused over the Ring's words, a sense of resolution settling within him. The time had come to reveal his alter ego to Layla, a disclosure that caused him considerable anxiety. It would be a step towards a new equilibrium, a bridge between his dual identities. But at least he would be honest, revealing the other side of himself to her.

For a brief moment, as he gazed across the city skyline, Simon felt an odd sensation—a prickling at the back of his neck, as if he were being watched from a great distance. The Fallen Ring seemed to pulse slightly on his finger, a barely perceptible vibration that travelled up his arm. He had the strange feeling like the sky was going to fall or something, an inexplicable sense of impending change.

Is something wrong? Simon directed the thought towards the Ring.

Perhaps nothing, came the uncertain reply. *Yet I sense … a disturbance. A familiarity I cannot place.*

Simon scanned the horizon once more but saw nothing unusual. The feeling passed as quickly as it had come, leaving only a vague unease in its wake.

A faint smile touched Simon's lips as he envisioned the conversations and revelations that lay ahead. He imagined Layla's reaction, the mingling of surprise, concern and hopefully understanding when he inevitably unveiled his secret. Through it all, he hoped for the strength to convey his intentions: to explore a life that balanced his commitment to justice with a life that retained some normalcy.

His contemplation was broken by a familiar sound. He reached into his pocket and retrieved the ringing phone. The caller ID displayed his mother's name.

'Hey, Mum.'

'Simon, dear, I hope I'm not interrupting anything.' Her voice was warm and comforting.

Simon's lips curved into a reassuring smile. 'Not at all, Mum. What's up?'

'Could you do me a favour, sweetheart? We're having a gathering at the house later, and I realised we're running low on drinks. Could you pick up a few things on your way back?'

Simon chuckled softly, the mundanity of the request grounding him completely from the currents of his contemplation. 'Of course, Mum. Anything specific you need?'

A list of items followed, each word spoken with a mother's love and attention to detail. As the conversation drew to a close, Simon's thoughts lingered on the task at hand. There was a sense of comfort in the mundane, a reminder that life's moments were composed of both ordinary and extraordinary thrills and challenges.

'I've got it, Mum. I'll see you soon,' he said with a cheerful smile.

Sliding his phone back into his pocket, he took a final look at the city spread out before him. The path ahead remained unknown, but in this moment, as he descended from the skyscraper and back into the embrace of the waking world, he carried a sense of purpose, one that extended beyond the shadow he cast as a vigilante.

As he made his way through Highbury and Islington, heading towards the shops his mother had mentioned, Simon passed a newsstand with stacks of free papers. His step faltered as his own eyes—or rather, the glowing purple eyes of his alter ego—stared back at him from the front page. "GUARDIAN STRIKES AGAIN" proclaimed the headline above a blurry image captured during last night's confrontation.

Simon picked up a copy, scanning the article with mixed emotions. His growing presence in the public eye wasn't something he'd planned for or particularly wanted. He preferred to work in the shadows, unrecognised and unhindered by fame or public scrutiny. And yet, seeing the impact of his actions documented this way stirred something in him—a small pride, perhaps, or simply the acknowledgment that his efforts were making a difference visible enough to be noticed.

He set the paper down with a slight smile and continued on his way. For Simon, London's silent protector, was on the precipice of a new chapter – one that he eagerly looked forward to.

CHAPTER 8

London pulsed with life beneath the cloud-streaked sky, its arteries congested with vehicles and pedestrians moving in their predictable patterns. From his vantage point high above the city, Eradax observed the rhythms of human existence with cold, analytical precision. His vessel, now in a stealth configuration that rendered it invisible to Earth's primitive detection systems, hovered silently over the metropolis.

'Fascinating,' Eradax murmured to himself as his sensors mapped the sprawling urban landscape below. 'Such disorder, yet somehow functional.'

The Ring's energy signature was stronger here, concentrated somewhere within this chaotic assembly of steel, glass, and stone. He could feel it—a subtle vibration in reality, calling to him like a beacon. But pinpointing its exact location was proving more challenging than anticipated. The signal seemed to shift, moving throughout the city rather than remaining stationary.

'The host is mobile,' he concluded, his crimson eyes narrowing. 'Active. Using the Ring's power.'

This complicated matters. A dormant Ring could simply be taken; an active one, bonded with a host, required a more ... deliberate approach. Eradax had not survived centuries of collecting the galaxy's most powerful artefacts by being reckless.

'Scan complete,' announced the ship's AI. 'Optimal location for concealment identified.'

A holographic display materialized before him, showing an abandoned industrial complex on London's eastern outskirts. Once a textile manufacturing facility, it had been vacant for years—forgotten by the humans who had built it, but perfect for Eradax's purposes. Isolated, structurally sound, and large enough to accommodate his vessel without drawing attention.

'Set course,' he commanded, his voice echoing in the empty command centre. 'Maintain stealth protocols.'

The vessel banked gently, moving away from the city centre and towards the neglected industrial zone. As they approached, Eradax studied the facility through multiple spectrums. No human presence detected within a half-kilometre radius. The building's roof had partially collapsed in one section, providing a convenient entry point for his ship.

The vessel descended silently through the opening, settling onto the concrete floor of what had once been the main production floor. Dust swirled in the air, disturbed for the first time in years. Massive, rusted machinery stood like silent sentinels, bearing witness to this otherworldly intrusion.

Eradax moved to the bridge viewscreen, his metallic form gleaming in the dim light of the ship's interior as he surveyed their new hiding place. Cloaked and concealed within this abandoned factory provided perfect cover—no one would think to look for advanced alien technology inside a derelict human structure.

'Activate perimeter sensors,' he instructed the ship's AI. 'Any human approach within 300 meters is to be flagged immediately.'

With the ship securely concealed and security measures in place, Eradax turned his attention to gathering intelligence. He activated a series of specialized drones—small, insect-like devices no larger than a human's thumb. They scattered, flying out through the ship's airlocks and then through broken windows and crevices of the factory, programmed to observe and record without being noticed.

'Interface with local information networks,' he commanded, moving to a terminal on the bridge. 'I require data on this city's inhabitants, governance, and defence systems.'

The display illuminated with a cascade of information as the ship's systems infiltrated Earth's digital infrastructure. Primitive by his standards, their security measures offered little resistance. Soon, the terminal displayed news outlets, government databases, and surveillance feeds from throughout the city.

Eradax's attention was drawn to recurring reports of an entity called "The Guardian." Multiple sources referenced this being—social media posts, news articles, police reports. A figure with glowing purple eyes who had been appearing throughout London, intervening in criminal activities.

'Display all available visual data on this "Guardian,"' he instructed.

The screen filled with blurry images and amateur video footage. Most were poor quality, captured in low light or from great distances. But there was enough for Eradax to make certain observations: the figure moved with inhuman speed and agility, demonstrated extraordinary strength, and appeared to be able to manipulate its physical form in ways that defied normal biology.

Most significant was the glow of the entity's eyes—a distinct purple hue that Eradax recognised immediately. The same energy signature as a Fallen Ring.

'So,' he said, his voice dropping to a contemplative tone, 'you have found a worthy host, have you?'

He studied the footage more carefully, noting how the Ring bearer seemed to conceal its true appearance, keeping to shadows and avoiding clear identification. Tactical. Cautious. Intelligent. This wasn't merely a human stumbling upon power—this was someone who understood its value and the importance of discretion.

One particular news report captured his attention. The headline read: "GUARDIAN FOILS ORPHANAGE ROBBERY, FOUR CRIMINALS ARRESTED." The article detailed how this vigilante had prevented the theft, pursuing and capturing a gang of professional thieves who had attempted to steal a substantial charitable donation.

'Fascinating,' Eradax murmured. 'The Ring bearer uses its power for protection. For justice.' The concept seemed almost amusing to him—such potential, such cosmic capability, directed towards such trivial ends. Noble, but inconsequential in the grand scheme of things.

His drones were returning now, one by one, docking in their designated ports within the ship and uploading their gathered data to the central system. Street layouts, population densities, security protocols of various facilities—all catalogued and analysed by his ship's computers. London was becoming known to him, its secrets unravelling with each passing moment.

Eradax moved to the observation port, a transparent section of the ship's hull that now faced one of the factory's high windows. From here, he could see the distant silhouette of London's skyline against the darkening evening sky. Somewhere in that urban expanse, the Fallen Ring awaited—its power calling to him across the kilometres.

'Begin compiling behavioural analysis,' he commanded. 'I want to know its patterns, its strengths, its weaknesses.'

As the system processed this request, Eradax remained at the viewport, his crimson eyes fixed on the city lights beginning to twinkle in the distance. His ship—his mobile fortress and laboratory—hummed softly around him, its advanced systems ready to serve whatever plan he would devise.

'Soon,' he promised, his metallic fingers curling into a fist. 'Soon you will join my collection, and your current bearer will be nothing but memory.'

The dust of the abandoned factory settled around the alien vessel, nature's shroud providing additional camouflage for the intruder that now waited within. To any passing human, the building would appear as nothing more than another decaying relic of a bygone industrial age. None would suspect that inside, one of the galaxy's most dangerous hunters had made Earth his latest hunting ground.

Eradax settled into patient observation. He had waited centuries to find a Fallen Ring; he could afford to be methodical now that one was within his grasp. The hunt was just beginning.

CHAPTER 9

Night had descended fully over London, the city now a canvas of artificial lights against darkness. Within his ship, concealed in the abandoned factory, Eradax stood motionless before a holographic display showing multiple streams of information simultaneously. News reports, security camera footage, police communications—all filtered through his advanced systems, each piece analysed and categorized according to relevance.

For three days, he had observed. Gathered. Learned.

The Ring bearer—this "Guardian," as the humans called him—was becoming a known entity to Eradax. His behavioural patterns were emerging: nocturnal activity predominately, focused on preventing criminal acts, a clear moral framework that guided his interventions. Fascinating, in its way, how such power had found its way to a being with such ... limitations of vision.

'Compile threat assessment,' Eradax commanded, his metallic digits manipulating the holographic controls with practiced precision.

The display shifted, consolidating data into a comprehensive profile. The Guardian possessed enhanced strength, extraordinary agility, apparent invulnerability to conventional weapons, and the ability to manipulate his physical form to some degree. All consistent with a Fallen Ring's capabilities, though clearly not utilizing its full potential.

'He has done more than merely scratch the surface of the Ring's power,' Eradax observed, studying the footage of the Guardian stopping a speeding vehicle with his bare hands. 'But the depths of what a Fallen Ring can truly achieve ... that iceberg goes far deeper than he has ventured. Such potential in the hands of one who has only begun to comprehend its true nature.'

He dismissed the display with a gesture and moved deeper into his vessel, towards a secured chamber that housed a fraction of his collection. The door slid open silently, revealing a room lined with containment units of varying sizes, each protecting an artefact of extraordinary nature. Some glowed with inner light, others seemed to absorb the illumination around them, creating pockets of shadow. All were unique, powerful, and dangerous in their own ways.

A Fallen Ring would be the crowning achievement in this collection—a prize he had sought for centuries but never managed to acquire.

Eradax approached a circular console at the room's centre, activating it with a touch. A holographic representation of a Ring materialized above it—not the one he sought, but a detailed model based on historical records and his own research.

'A most fascinating symbiosis of sentience and power,' he said softly, studying the projection. 'Capable of unlocking realities beyond mortal comprehension.'

His crimson eyes narrowed as he considered his approach. Direct confrontation would be ... inefficient. The Ring bearer was powerful, perhaps even a match for Eradax's own considerable abilities. Unnecessary risk was the hallmark of a failed collector, and Eradax had not survived this long by being careless.

No, a more elegant strategy was required. One that would not only secure the Ring but provide ... entertainment. After all, what value was there in a simple acquisition? The art was in the pursuit, in the game of intellect and will that preceded possession.

Eradax returned to the bridge, calling up the report on the orphanage robbery that had caught his attention earlier. The four humans involved—their images displayed prominently in the news coverage—had been arrested and now resided in a facility the humans called a "prison." A primitive containment structure, barely worth the name by his standards.

'Access Earth judicial database,' he instructed. 'Locate records for these individuals.'

The ship's AI complied instantly, infiltrating the secure systems with ease. Soon, detailed profiles appeared before him:

Dushane Barracks. Leader. Tactical mind. Multiple prior offenses, all executed fastidiously.

Wei Zhang. Technical specialist. Expert in security systems and locks. Methodical approach to criminal enterprises.

Mateo Reyes. Physical enforcer. Enhanced strength through stolen mechanical exoskeleton technology, though primitive by galactic standards.

Callum Briggs. The newest member of their group. Less experienced, but demonstrated adaptability under pressure.

'Interesting,' Eradax murmured, studying their histories. 'A well-balanced team. Specialized skills. And a personal grudge against the Guardian, if their capture was as ... humiliating as reported.'

The beginnings of a plan formed in his mind—a strategy that would serve multiple purposes. These humans could be useful tools, pawns to be positioned carefully on the board. Their existing skills, enhanced by his technology, could create a formidable challenge for the Ring bearer. Not enough to defeat him, perhaps, but sufficient to reveal the full extent of his capabilities. To force him to draw deeper on the Ring's power.

Such a confrontation would serve three purposes: testing the Guardian's limits, weakening him through extended conflict, and providing Eradax with the entertainment he craved. After all, the hunt was always more satisfying when it included an element of sport.

'Access storage vault inventory,' Eradax commanded. 'Display combat enhancement technology suitable for human augmentation.'

The screen before him filled with schematics for devices collected from a dozen different worlds—weapons, armour, neural interfaces, genetic modifiers. Each piece a marvel by Earth standards, representing technologies centuries or millennia beyond their current capabilities.

Eradax studied the options, considering how each might be adapted to the specific abilities of the four humans. For Dushane, perhaps the shockwave blasters from the Krell civilisation. For Wei, the gravitational manipulation harness, enabling flight. For Mateo, an advanced powered exoskeleton with integrated armour—a significant upgrade to the primitive version he had used before. And for Callum, some bioelectric channelling gauntlets that would allow him to conduct and blast electricity—a weapon that would make him formidable.

'Perfect,' he said, the word carrying a cold satisfaction. 'How will this Ring bearer fare against this fearsome four, each armed with significant upgrades?'

But the equipment was only part of the equation. These humans would need motivation, direction. The prison break itself wouldn't be much of a problem—Earth's security systems were laughably inadequate compared to his ship's capabilities. But ensuring their cooperation, their focus ... that would require a more personal touch.

Eradax activated a secondary display, showing the layout of the prison facility where the four were being held. Security systems, guard rotations, structural vulnerabilities—all catalogued and analysed by his ship's computers.

'The timing must be precise,' he mused. 'Their release must appear to be their own achievement, their enhanced capabilities special gifts. They must not understand the true nature of their benefactor until I choose to reveal myself.'

He considered the psychological profiles his system had compiled. Dushane's pride and tactical mind made him the obvious focal point. Appeal to his desire for revenge, his need to reclaim status, and the others would follow his lead naturally.

'How amusing,' Eradax said, a cold approximation of humour in his metallic voice. 'To use their primitive emotions as precisely as I will use their enhanced abilities.'

The ship's lighting dimmed slightly as energy was redirected to the fabrication systems, preparing the selected technologies for deployment. It would take time to adapt them for human use—simplifying interfaces, ensuring compatibility with their biology, adding safeguards that would prevent them from turning against their benefactor.

Eradax moved to the viewport once more, looking out towards the distant glow of London's centre. Somewhere in that metropolis, the Ring bearer continued his self-appointed mission, unaware of the trap being laid.

'Enjoy your power while you can, Guardian,' he said to the distant lights. 'Soon you will understand what it means to face a true collector of relics.'

He turned away from the window, his mind settled on the strategy ahead. This approach would provide valuable data on the Ring bearer's capabilities while simultaneously testing potential weaknesses. And if these human pawns failed? Nothing lost but tools that had served their purpose.

Either way, Eradax would be entertained. And closer to claiming his prize.

The hunt had entered its next phase.

CHAPTER 10

The harsh fluorescent lights of HMP Belmarsh buzzed overhead, casting everything in a sickly pale glow that made even the youngest inmates look haggard and worn. Dushane Barracks sat perfectly still on the edge of his bunk, his expression impassive as he stared at the wall opposite him. Two weeks. Two weeks since the Guardian had ripped away everything—their score, their freedom, their reputation.

'Barracks! Visitor.'

The guard's voice cut through his thoughts. Dushane stood without a word, allowing himself to be escorted down the corridor, past rows of cells identical to his own. The routine was familiar now—hands out for cuffs, turn, walk, stop, wait for doors to open, continue. Simple. Degrading.

The visitors' area was crowded that day, filled with the low murmur of conversations carefully monitored by watchful guards. Dushane spotted a familiar face already seated at one of the tables—Javon, his cousin and occasional business associate, a man who had managed to stay just clean enough to avoid police attention.

'They got you good this time,' Javon said as Dushane took the seat opposite him.

'How're the others?' Dushane asked, cutting straight to what mattered.

'Wei and Mateo are in the same block, B-wing. Callum's in C-wing. Mateo's already in isolation after he put two inmates in the infirmary yesterday.'

'Sounds like him,' Dushane said, a flicker of pride crossing his features. Mateo had never been one to roll over, prison or no prison. 'What about the case?'

Javon leaned forward slightly, lowering his voice. 'Prosecutor's building a case on the physical evidence. The money recovered at the scene. The damage to the orphanage. The modified Jeep registered to one of your shell companies.' His face darkened. 'They're talking fifteen years, minimum.'

Dushane absorbed this without visible reaction, though his fists clenched involuntarily on the table. Fifteen years. A decade and a half stolen from him by a freak in a crazy costume.

'Have you talked to Richards?' he asked, referring to their longtime lawyer.

'Yesterday. He's trying to get the evidence thrown out—arguing chain of custody was broken when the Guardian interfered. Standard stuff. But ...' Javon trailed off, his expression grim.

'But it won't work,' Dushane finished for him. 'Not with the amount of bags they recovered.'

Their conversation paused as a guard passed nearby, resuming only when the man had moved to the other side of the room.

'I've been talking with the others,' Javon said quietly. 'About him. The Guardian.'

Dushane's eyes narrowed. 'What about him?'

'Wei says he's not normal. What he did to Mateo's exo-suit ... that wasn't human strength. And the way he moved—' Javon shook his head. 'According to Wei, it wasn't like anything he's ever seen before.'

'So what? He's got some fancy tech or he's on something. Doesn't make him untouchable.'

Javon studied Dushane carefully. 'You're planning something.'

It wasn't a question, and Dushane didn't treat it as one. Instead, he leaned back slightly, his gaze drifting to the ceiling as if considering his next words carefully.

'When we get out of here—and we will get out, one way or another—we find him. We figure out what makes him tick. And then we break him,' Dushane said, his voice flat and matter-of-fact. 'No one humiliates us and walks away. No one.'

Javon's expression remained neutral, but Dushane caught the slight nod of agreement. 'I'll let the others know. Wei's already working on something from the inside.'

'Time's up,' called a guard from the door. 'Back to your cells.'

Dushane stood without protest, allowing the guard to reapply his cuffs. As he was led away, he glanced back at

Javon, who gave him a barely perceptible nod. The message was clear: this conversation would continue.

***

The yard was Dushane's least favourite place in Belmarsh. Too exposed, too many eyes watching, too many potential conflicts brewing in the tense interactions between rival groups. But it was also the only place he could reliably meet Callum these days, with the prison administration having separated them into different blocks.

He found the youngest member of his team by the weight bench, his lean frame already showing the results of prison workout routines. Survival in here required strength—physical and otherwise.

'Boss,' Callum acknowledged him, setting down the weights. 'Thought they might keep you in solitary after yesterday.'

Dushane shrugged. 'Guard decided not to report it. Seems he's not a big fan of child molesters either.'

The man who had made the mistake of threatening Dushane in the showers had learned a painful lesson about hierarchy. Dushane might be new to Belmarsh, but he wasn't new to establishing respect.

'You hear about Mateo?' Callum asked, lowering his voice.

'Javon told me. Isolation.'

'Third time this month.' There was a note of admiration in Callum's voice. 'Guards are talking about transferring him to a higher security wing.'

Dushane frowned. Having Mateo moved would complicate things. They needed to be able to communicate, to plan. His gaze swept across the yard, cataloguing positions of guards, cameras, potential listeners.

'You been keeping your head down?' he asked.

Callum nodded. 'Just like you said. No trouble, no attention.'

'Good.' Dushane leaned against the weight bench, keeping his voice casual. 'I need you to get a message to Wei when you see him in the mess hall. Tell him to look into the electrical systems in C-block. The lights have been flickering. Might be useful.'

Callum's eyes widened slightly with understanding. Wei, their technician, would know what to look for—weaknesses, blind spots, opportunities. Every prison had them; it was just a matter of finding the right ones.

'And Callum,' Dushane added, fixing the younger man with an intense stare. 'You remember what he took from us?'

'The Guardian?' Callum's expression hardened. 'Every night when I'm staring at the ceiling in that cell.'

'Good. Keep that anger. We're going to need it.'

A whistle blew, signalling the end of yard time. Inmates began shuffling towards the doors, forming into orderly lines under the watchful eyes of guards.

'What about you, Boss?' Callum asked as they joined the procession. 'How are you holding up?'

Dushane's face remained impassive, but his eyes burned with quiet intensity. 'I'm planning. Every minute of every day.'

***

The prison library was nearly empty when Dushane entered. Just how he liked it. He nodded to the elderly librarian who barely acknowledged his presence before heading to the far corner where newspapers were kept. It had become part of his routine—scanning through every publication for any mention of the Guardian.

Today's Evening Standard had a small article on page three: 'Guardian Rescues Family From Apartment Fire.' Next to it, another headline: 'Masked Vigilante Thwarts Armed Robbery in Soho.' Dushane read both articles twice, carefully committing details to memory. The vigilante's pattern was pretty clear—nocturnal activities most of the time, but appearing whenever people were in danger, seemingly random appearances across London.

But nothing was truly random. There would be a pattern, a home base, a weakness. Everyone had one.

As he replaced the newspaper, Dushane noticed an unfamiliar inmate watching him from across the room. The man was tall, well-built, with the hard eyes of someone who had seen his share of violence. After a moment's hesitation, the stranger approached.

'Barracks, right?' the man asked quietly. 'The one who hit the orphanage.'

Dushane stood his ground, measuring the potential threat. 'Who's asking?'

'Name's Miller.' The man glanced around before continuing. 'Word is you've got a particular interest in our purple-eyed friend out there.'

Dushane's expression didn't change, but his attention sharpened. 'What about it?'

'I've seen him. Up close. Before he became front-page news.' Miller's voice dropped even lower. 'There's something wrong about him. Not natural.'

'You're not telling me anything I don't already know,' Dushane replied dismissively.

Miller leaned closer. 'There are others interested in him too. People with resources. People who might look favourably on anyone who could ... provide information.'

Dushane considered the man carefully. A plant? Possible. A trap? Also possible. But the mention of "others" with "resources" was too intriguing to dismiss outright.

'I'm listening,' he said finally.

'Strange things have been happening in the prison,' Miller continued. 'Computer glitches. Security cameras going offline for seconds at a time. The kind of things most people wouldn't notice.'

'And you're what? An expert in prison security systems?'

Miller smiled thinly. 'I was in cybersecurity before a ... career change. Old habits die hard.' He tapped his temple. 'Keep your eyes open, Barracks. Opportunity doesn't always announce itself.'

Before Dushane could press further, a guard called out that library time was over. Miller gave him a meaningful look before melting back into the small crowd of inmates heading for the exit.

Dushane followed, his mind racing. The conversation had left him with more questions than answers, but one thing was becoming increasingly clear: something was happening inside Belmarsh. Something that might align perfectly with his own ambitions.

Back in his cell, as the door clanged shut behind him, Dushane lay on his bunk and stared at the ceiling. The Guardian's glowing purple eyes seemed to float in his memory, a constant reminder of his humiliation. But for the first time since his arrest, Dushane felt something beyond rage.

He felt hope.

Strange things happening in the prison. Security glitches. Others with resources and interest in the Guardian.

Perhaps the universe was finally tilting back in his favour.

As the lights dimmed for lockdown, Dushane allowed himself a small smile. The Guardian might have won their first encounter, but the game was far from over. And this time, when they met again, things would end very differently.

Of that, Dushane Barracks was absolutely certain.

Chapter 11

— · —

The night guard's footsteps echoed through B-wing, the rhythmic sound of his boots against concrete marking time like a metronome. Wei Zhang lay motionless on his bunk, eyes fixed on the ceiling, counting the seconds between each pass. Eighteen minutes for a complete circuit—predictable, like most security systems. People were always the weakest link.

Three cells down, he knew Mateo would be doing the same, waiting for the signal they had discussed in hushed tones during yesterday's brief yard meeting. Across the prison in C-wing, Callum would be counting too. Dushane had set everything in motion during mealtime earlier, a simple nod conveying that tonight was the night.

Wei closed his eyes, recalling the strange electrical fluctuations he'd been monitoring for the past week. The prison's lighting system would dim for precisely 3.7 seconds at intervals that seemed random at first, but after careful observation, he'd identified a pattern. Every third night, between 2:15 and 2:20 AM, the anomaly would affect the surveillance system as well. A minor glitch most would overlook—but Wei wasn't most people.

Something was interfering with Belmarsh's systems. Or someone.

The cell block's lights flickered once, briefly. Wei opened his eyes. Almost time.

He slipped from his bunk and moved to the small metal sink in the corner of his cell. Reaching beneath it, his fingers found the loose panel he'd carefully worked free over several nights. From this hidden space, he retrieved a small device cobbled together from parts scavenged throughout the prison—a crude electromagnetic pulse generator built from a modified radio, some copper wire from the workshop, and components from several smuggled mobile phones.

Not his finest work, but it would serve its purpose.

The digital clock in the corridor outside his cell read 2:14 AM.

Wei positioned himself by the door, device in hand, and waited.

*****

In the isolation wing, Mateo Reyes sat with his back against the wall, methodically flexing each muscle group to stay loose. The guards had searched his cell twice today, unusual even by isolation standards. They'd found nothing, of course. The small shiv he'd crafted wasn't hidden in his cell at all, but taped beneath the underside of the meal trolley that would arrive for breakfast in a few hours.

Not that he expected to be here for breakfast.

Mateo's eyes drifted to the ventilation grate near the ceiling. Too small for most men to fit through, but the maintenance access panel in the shower block was another story. He'd noticed it during his supervised shower time yesterday—poorly secured, recently serviced according to the maintenance log still attached. An oversight that would cost the prison dearly.

When the lights dimmed slightly, Mateo's posture straightened. One flicker. Soon there would be another. And then, chaos.

***

Callum Briggs was the newest to prison life among Dushane's crew, but what he lacked in experience, he made up for in nerve. As he lay in his cell in C-wing, a thin blanket covering the shape he'd constructed from his spare clothes and bedding, his heart hammered against his ribs.

He wasn't in his cell at all, but wedged into the narrow space behind the industrial washing machine in the laundry room, where he'd hidden himself during his work detail. The guard's cursory count at lockdown had been fooled by the dummy in his bed—a trick that would buy him hours before the next proper check.

When the laundry room's lights flickered, Callum began counting under his breath. If Wei's observations were correct, the second flicker would come within thirty seconds, and then they'd have their window.

Twenty-eight. Twenty-nine. Thirty.

The lights dimmed again, longer this time. Callum slipped out from his hiding place and moved towards the service door, retrieving the keycard he'd managed to clone using equipment smuggled in by a corrupt orderly whom Dushane had connections with on the outside.

Everything was falling into place.

***

In D-wing, Dushane sat calmly on the edge of his bunk, fully dressed despite the late hour. Unlike his associates, he had made no preparations, gathered no tools, planned no route. His role was simply to be ready.

When the lights in his cell flickered for the second time, he stood and walked to the centre of the small space. The digital clock on the wall outside his cell froze at 2:17, its display stuttering before going dark.

'Right on time,' Dushane murmured to himself.

At precisely 2:18 AM, every electronic lock in Belmarsh Prison simultaneously disengaged with a synchronized metallic click.

***

Wei heard it first—the soft electronic tone of the cell door control system resetting, followed by the unmistakable sound of locks releasing throughout the wing. Not just his door, but every door. Exactly as he had predicted after studying the pattern of electrical anomalies.

What he hadn't predicted was that he wouldn't need his makeshift EMP device at all.

Confused voices rose from other cells as inmates realized their doors were unlocked. Wei didn't hesitate. He slipped from his cell and moved swiftly down the corridor towards the predetermined meeting point—the maintenance junction where B-wing connected to the main administrative block. Guards were already shouting, but the confusion was working in their favour.

He turned a corner and nearly collided with Mateo, who had moved with surprising speed from isolation.

'How did you—' Wei began.

'Maintenance panel,' Mateo replied curtly, his large frame blocking most of the narrow corridor. 'Where's Callum?'

'If he stuck to the plan, he'll meet us at the junction.'

Alarms began to blare, their piercing wail adding to the growing chaos. The sound of running footsteps and shouting echoed from multiple directions.

'We need to move,' Mateo said, already turning towards their escape route.

***

Callum had never considered himself particularly lucky, but tonight, fortune seemed determined to smile upon him. The laundry room's service door had opened with the cloned keycard, and the utility corridor beyond was deserted. The alarms were sounding, but in this section of the prison, they seemed distant, almost muffled.

He navigated the maintenance passages as Wei had instructed him, counting doorways until he reached the junction point. Voices approached from his left—guards, from the sound of it, rushing to respond to what they likely assumed was a technical malfunction rather than a coordinated escape.

Callum pressed himself into a shadowed alcove, holding his breath as two uniformed officers rushed past. When they had gone, he continued forward, emerging into the wider corridor that connected the prison's various wings. Ahead, he could see the maintenance junction—and two familiar figures already waiting.

'Wei! Mateo!' he called in a harsh whisper, jogging towards them.

Wei acknowledged him with a quick nod. 'Dushane?'

'Haven't seen him,' Callum replied.

'He'll be here,' Mateo said with certainty.

As if summoned by the words, a fourth figure appeared from the shadows of a connecting hallway, moving with the calm purpose of a man taking a casual stroll rather than escaping a maximum-security prison.

'Gentlemen,' Dushane greeted them, as if they were meeting for a business deal rather than a prison break. 'Shall we?'

***

The four men moved through the maintenance corridors with practiced coordination, following the route Wei had meticulously planned based on his observations and the stolen glimpses of architectural plans he'd managed to view during a supervised library visit.

'The emergency exit near the kitchen loading bay is our best bet,' Wei explained as they navigated the labyrinthine service passages. 'The locks are electronic, so they should be affected by whatever caused the system-wide failure.'

'And if they're not?' Callum asked.

'Then Mateo makes us a new door,' Dushane replied simply.

As they approached the final corridor leading to the exit, the sound of the alarms grew louder. Guards would be everywhere by now, trying to contain what had become a prison-wide disruption. Not just their planned escape, but dozens of opportunistic inmates taking advantage of the unlocked doors.

The perfect cover.

Wei held up a hand, signalling them to stop as they reached the final corner. Peering around it carefully, he could see the emergency exit at the end of the hall-way—and two guards stationed in front of it, weapons drawn.

'Two at the door,' he whispered, drawing back.

'Armed?' Dushane asked.

Wei nodded.

Mateo flexed his massive hands. 'Not a problem.'

'No,' Dushane said firmly. 'No casualties. We need clean getaway, not a murder charge.'

Before they could formulate a plan, the lights in the corridor ahead flickered again—once, twice, and then went out completely, plunging the area into darkness. They heard confused shouts from the guards, then the sound of a door opening.

'What's happening?' Callum whispered.

'Our opportunity,' Dushane replied, his voice steady in the darkness. 'Move. Now.'

Taking advantage of the blackout, the four men rushed forward, navigating by touch along the wall. Wei reached the emergency exit first, finding it standing partially open. The guards who had been stationed there were gone, presumably to investigate the power failure.

'It's clear,' he called softly to the others.

One by one, they slipped through the door into the cool night air of the loading bay. The prison's perimeter was still some distance away, but the power outage had affected the floodlights as well. The yard was cast in shadows, broken only by the sweeping beams of emergency spotlights operated by increasingly frantic guards on the walls.

'The fence,' Wei pointed to their left, where the loading area connected to a service road. 'There's a section near the garbage disposal area where we can climb over.'

They moved quickly across the open space, using shipping containers and parked vehicles for cover. The prison was in full emergency mode now, sirens wailing and spotlights scanning the grounds, but most of the attention seemed focused on containing the inmates inside rather than those who had already made it this far.

As they reached the section of fence Wei had indicated, Mateo went first, his powerful arms making quick work of the climb despite the barbed wire at the top. He dropped down on the other side, then gestured for the others to follow.

One by one, they scaled the fence, Callum wincing as the barbed wire caught and tore his prison uniform. Dushane came last, his movements deliberate and unhurried even as a spotlight swept dangerously close to their position.

Once all four were over, they sprinted for the cover of trees beyond the service road. Behind them, the prison was a cacophony of alarms and shouted orders, but no pursuit seemed immediately forthcoming. The chaos within the prison walls was working exactly as Dushane had anticipated.

'That way,' Dushane pointed further into the trees once they had caught their breath. 'Javon said he'd leave a vehicle near the old service station on Woolwich Road.'

'How far?' Mateo asked.

'Two miles, cross-country,' Dushane replied. 'We need to move quickly. When they realize we're gone, this entire area will be locked down.'

As they began to move through the darkness, following Dushane's lead, Callum voiced the question that had been in all their minds.

'What just happened back there? Those power failures ... that wasn't normal. The whole security system just ... gave up.'

Wei nodded in agreement. 'I've been monitoring the glitches for days. They were too precise, too coordinated. Someone helped us. Someone with access to advanced technology.'

'The question is who,' Mateo added. 'And why.'

Dushane said nothing, his eyes fixed on the path ahead, but his mind was racing. Someone had orchestrated their escape—someone with the power to override one of Britain's most secure prisons. Someone who wanted them free.

The implications were both troubling and intriguing.

'Whoever it was,' he finally said, 'I suspect we'll find out soon enough. For now, we focus on putting distance between us and Belmarsh.'

The four men continued through the darkness, leaving the chaos of the prison behind them. Freedom lay ahead—and with it, the promise of revenge against the Guardian who had put them there.

None of them noticed the small drone hovering silently among the branches above, its red optical sensor tracking their every move as they disappeared into the night.

CHAPTER 12

Late morning sun filtered through a heavy blanket of fog that shrouded the abandoned industrial complex. The rusted hulk of the old chemical plant had been derelict for nearly a decade, its crumbling walls adorned with graffiti and its grounds overtaken by weeds pushing through cracked concrete. It was the perfect place to disappear.

Dushane stood by the grimy window of what had once been a foreman's office, watching as police helicopters circled in the distance. The news of their escape had broken hours ago, dominating every radio broadcast and news channel. Four dangerous criminals on the loose, armed and desperate—that was the official line being fed to the public. In reality, they were exhausted, hungry, and acutely aware of their vulnerability.

'How much longer?' Mateo asked, his massive frame leaning against a wall, arms crossed over his chest. The others were scattered around the room—Wei busy with a stolen laptop, attempting to secure communications, and Callum nervously pacing back and forth.

'Javon said noon,' Dushane replied, checking his watch. 'Someone's coming with new IDs, money, and transport out of the country.'

Wei looked up from his laptop, his expression troubled. 'It still doesn't add up. The prison break … it wasn't just luck. The entire security system failed simultaneously. That's military-grade interference.'

'You think MI5 broke us out?' Callum asked with a nervous laugh.

'No,' Wei replied seriously. 'I think someone with resources far beyond what we're accustomed to wanted us out of Belmarsh. The question is why.'

Dushane turned from the window. 'Does it matter? We're out. We're free. Now we can focus on what's important.'

'The Guardian,' Mateo growled, his fists clenching involuntarily.

'Exactly,' Dushane confirmed. 'But first, we need to get clear of this manhunt.'

Wei returned his attention to the laptop, then suddenly froze. 'That's … impossible.'

'What?' Dushane moved to look over his shoulder.

'Someone's overriding my security protocols. They're—'

Before he could finish, the laptop screen went blank, then filled with a single line of text:

REMAIN WHERE YOU ARE. ASSISTANCE ARRIVES AT 12:17.

The four men exchanged wary glances.

'It's 12:15 now,' Callum said, checking his watch.

'Could be the police,' Mateo suggested, moving to the doorway to watch the entrance.

'No,' Wei shook his head. 'This isn't police. This is something else entirely.'

They waited in tense silence, seconds ticking by with excruciating slowness. At exactly 12:17, the air in the centre of the room seemed to shimmer, like heat rising from sun-baked asphalt. The distortion grew, expanding outward until it formed a swirling vortex of light that cast strange shadows across the walls.

Callum stumbled backwards with a strangled cry. Mateo raised his fists defensively. Wei stared in scientific fascination. Dushane remained perfectly still, his face an impassive mask despite the impossibility unfolding before them.

From the centre of the light emerged a figure that defied explanation—a towering entity of gleaming metal and crimson eyes, humanoid in basic form but unmistakably alien. The light collapsed behind it, leaving the room in semi-darkness once more except for the faint glow emanating from the being's eyes.

'Gentlemen,' the entity said, its voice a metallic rasp that seemed to reverberate inside their skulls. 'I am Eradax, the Collector of Relics. And I have a proposition for you.'

Mateo was the first to react, lunging forward with surprising speed for a man of his size. But before he could make contact, he found himself frozen in place, held by some invisible force that rendered him immobile. An iridescent crystal in Eradax's palm pulsed with shifting colours as the alien casually held up his hand.

'I would advise against such actions,' Eradax said calmly, the crystal's otherworldly glow subsiding as he closed his fist. 'Had I wished you harm, you would not have made it this far.'

With a casual gesture, he released Mateo, who staggered back, his expression a mixture of rage and bewilderment.

'What the hell are you?' Callum whispered.

'A visitor to your world,' Eradax replied. 'One with interests that currently align with your own.'

Dushane stepped forward, unfazed by the alien presence. 'You broke us out of Belmarsh.'

It wasn't a question, but Eradax inclined his head in acknowledgment. 'A simple matter of overriding primitive security systems. Your escape was ... convenient to my purposes.'

'What purposes?' Wei asked, his analytical mind already recovering from the shock.

Eradax's crimson gaze shifted to him. 'The being you know as the Guardian. The one who defeated you, imprisoned you. The one you seek to destroy.'

Dushane's eyes narrowed. 'What's your interest in him?'

'He possesses something I desire. An artefact of great value.' Eradax made a dismissive gesture. 'The details are irrelevant to our arrangement. What matters is that we share a common adversary.'

'So you want us to, what, kill him for you?' Mateo asked bluntly.

'Not necessarily.' Eradax moved around the room with a strange grace, his metallic form reflecting the dim light. 'I want you to challenge him. Test his limits. Wear him

down. And in exchange, I offer you the means to do so …
and much more.'

With a fluid motion, the alien raised his hand, revealing
a small device that projected a holographic display into the
centre of the room. Four distinct sets of advanced technology appeared, rotating slowly in the air before them—each
clearly designed for combat, each radiating power beyond
anything they had encountered before.

'I have studied each of you,' Eradax continued. 'Your capabilities. Your potential. Your particular … talents. What
I offer is not merely weaponry, but tools that will enhance
your natural abilities, making you formidable opponents.'

The holographic display shifted, focusing on the first set
of equipment—gauntlets and a chest piece adorned with
intricate circuitry.

'For Dushane Barracks, the strategist: shockwave
blasters capable of shattering concrete and steel alike.
Control over concussive force, both focused and dis-
persed.'

The display shifted again.

'For Wei Zhang, the technician: a gravity harness with
razor-sharp wings. Flight capabilities. Aerial supremacy.
The sharpened tips provide lethal offensive capabilities.'

Another shift, revealing a massive exoskeleton.

'For Mateo Reyes, the enforcer: advanced power armour, exponentially enhancing your already formidable
strength while providing near-impenetrable protection.'

The final display showed a sleek, form-fitting suit laced
with conductive material.

'And for Callum Briggs, the adaptable one: bioelectric channelling technology. The ability to conduct, store, and discharge massive electrical currents.'

The holograms faded, leaving the room dimmer than before. The four men stood in stunned silence, the implications of what they were being offered sinking in.

'Why would you give us this?' Dushane finally asked, his voice level despite the magnitude of the situation. 'What's your real angle?'

Eradax's metallic features formed what might have been a smile. 'Consider it an experiment. I wish to observe the Guardian's capabilities when faced with worthy opponents. And you wish for revenge. Our goals complement each other perfectly.'

'And what happens after?' Wei asked. 'Assuming we survive a confrontation with him?'

'The technology remains yours,' Eradax replied. 'To use as you see fit. This world would be open to you in ways you can barely imagine.'

Dushane exchanged glances with his crew. The offer was beyond tempting—it was transformative. Not just revenge against the Guardian, but power that would elevate them far beyond their former criminal enterprises.

'We need to discuss this,' he said finally.

'Of course,' Eradax agreed, stepping back. 'Though I should mention that the authorities are currently expanding their search radius. Within approximately forty-three minutes, this facility will be within their operational perimeter.'

Dushane led the others to the far corner of the room, their heads close together as they spoke in hushed tones.

'This is insane,' Callum hissed. 'He's a bloody alien! How do we know he won't just kill us once we've done what he wants?'

'We don't,' Wei admitted. 'But consider the alternative. On our own, with the entire country looking for us, how far do we get? How close do we come to the Guardian?'

Mateo's eyes were fixed on the alien across the room. 'I want that armour,' he said simply. 'I want to crush him like he crushed us.'

Dushane remained silent for a moment, weighing their options. Freedom with uncertain prospects, or power with uncertain allies. The choice, when framed that way, was obvious.

'We accept,' he announced, turning back to Eradax. 'But we do this our way. We're not your soldiers.'

'I would expect nothing less,' Eradax replied. 'Your independence is precisely what makes you valuable. Now, shall we depart? My facility is considerably more ... comfortable than your current accommodations.'

With another gesture, the air in the centre of the room began to shimmer once more. This time, the distortion expanded into what appeared to be a portal, through which they could see a cavernous metallic chamber unlike anything earthly architecture could produce.

'After you,' Eradax invited.

One by one, they stepped through—first Wei, propelled by scientific curiosity; then Mateo, drawn by the promise of power; followed by Callum, unwilling to be left behind.

Dushane paused at the threshold, giving one last look at the world they were leaving behind.

When he stepped through, the portal collapsed behind them, leaving no trace that they had ever been there.

CHAPTER 13

The interior of Eradax's vessel was beyond anything Dushane and his crew could have imagined. Sleek metallic surfaces housed technology that seemed to operate on principles that defied Earth's physics. Holographic displays appeared and disappeared at the alien's command, showing landscapes and beings from worlds they had never dreamed existed.

'This will be your sanctuary while you prepare,' Eradax explained as he led them through corridors that seemed to shift and reconfigure with each turn. 'Undetectable by your world's surveillance systems, beyond the reach of your authorities.'

They arrived at a vast chamber where the four sets of equipment they had seen in hologram form now stood on display, each on its own illuminated platform.

'These are not merely weapons,' Eradax cautioned as they approached the platforms. 'They are sophisticated tools designed to amplify your existing capabilities. The controls are intuitive, designed to be mastered quickly.'

Dushane moved towards the gauntlets and chest piece designed for him, his hand hovering over the surface without touching. 'How long to learn how to use them effectively?'

'Hours for basic functionality,' Eradax replied. 'Days for advanced techniques. The interfaces are designed to be as seamless as possible. You'll find yourselves formidable opponents for the Guardian much sooner than you might expect.'

Wei was already examining the gravitational harness, his analytical mind working to understand its principles. 'This technology ... it's centuries beyond anything on Earth.'

'Millennia, by your measurements,' Eradax corrected. 'But designed to be operated by human users nonetheless.'

Mateo stood before the massive exoskeleton, his eyes gleaming with anticipation. 'When do we start?'

'Immediately,' Eradax said. 'The sooner you familiarize yourselves with the equipment, the sooner you can begin your campaign against the Guardian.'

As the others moved to their respective platforms, drawn like moths to flame, Dushane remained slightly apart, his gaze calculating. The pieces of a plan already forming in his mind. They would need time to master these new tools, to develop strategies that played to their collective strengths. But more than that, they would need an identity—something to strike fear into the heart of their enemy, to announce their return to the city. One that it wouldn't forget.

'The Reclaimers,' he said suddenly, the name coming to him with perfect clarity.

The others turned to look at him.

'The what?' Callum asked.

'That's who we are now,' Dushane said, his voice carrying a newfound authority. 'We're going to reclaim what was taken from us ... and then some. The whole world will be our oyster when we're done.'

Mateo grinned, the name clearly resonating with him. Wei nodded his approval. Even Callum seemed to stand taller at the declaration.

'The Reclaimers,' Eradax repeated, his metallic voice carrying an undertone of satisfaction. 'How ... appropriate.'

As they began examining their new equipment, each man approaching their platform with a mixture of caution and eagerness, Dushane felt a sense of power and purpose unlike anything he had ever experienced. The Guardian had beaten them once, when they were merely men with conventional weapons. But they were becoming something far more dangerous now.

And London would tremble at their return.

***

From his position overlooking the chamber, Eradax observed the transformation with cold calculation. These humans were proving to be perfect tools—driven by revenge, eager for power, and completely unaware of their true purpose in his grand design. By the time they realized they were merely pawns in a larger game, their usefulness would already be fulfilled.

The hunt for the Fallen Ring had entered its most interesting phase.

CHAPTER 14

Simon logged out of his terminal at precisely 4:00 PM, rolling his shoulders to ease the tension that had built up over a day of hunting vulnerabilities in his client's network infrastructure. Six weeks into his new position at Sentinel Cybersecurity, and he was already making a name for himself—the quiet consultant who could spot system weaknesses that veteran analysts missed.

'Heading out on time on a Friday? Must be something special,' remarked Priya, his team lead, as she passed his desk.

Simon smiled, tucking his laptop into his messenger bag. 'Dinner plans.'

'The mysterious girlfriend?' Priya raised an eyebrow. 'The one none of us have ever seen? I'm starting to think you made her up.'

'Layla's real,' Simon assured her with a good-natured laugh. 'Just busy with her work at the NHS Trust.'

'Well, enjoy your weekend. Try not to think about code for at least forty-eight hours.'

Simon nodded, though they both knew he'd likely be reviewing security protocols before Sunday night. That, and delving deeper into financial literacy—an area he approached with the same methodical focus he gave to code. It wasn't just about numbers or spreadsheets; it was a calculated step towards securing his future. Doing this often helped quiet his mind when the weight of his double life grew heavy.

Outside, London's early evening was surprisingly pleasant for early autumn, golden light slanting between buildings as commuters streamed towards tube stations and buses. Simon checked his watch and decided to walk part of the way, cutting through side streets towards the Turkish restaurant near Green Lanes where he'd arranged to meet Layla.

As he walked, his mind drifted to the news he'd seen during lunch—a reminder of the prison break at Belmarsh some weeks ago. The four criminals he'd apprehended at the orphanage had somehow escaped, along with several other inmates during what authorities were calling a "catastrophic security system failure." The police had no leads, which struck Simon as particularly odd. Men like Dushane Barracks didn't simply vanish.

You're concerned, the Fallen Ring observed in his mind.

Wouldn't you be? Simon thought back. *Four dangerous criminals with a personal grudge against the Guardian, suddenly in the wind.*

We'll find them, the Ring replied with its characteristic certainty. *But perhaps not tonight.*

Simon nodded slightly to himself. Tonight was for Layla. Tomorrow he'd begin tracking the escapees.

The restaurant was busy when he arrived, the aroma of grilled meat and spices spilling onto the sidewalk as the door opened and closed. Through the window, he spotted Layla already seated at a corner table, her dark chestnut hair falling in waves around her shoulders as she studied something on her phone. The sight of her sent a familiar warmth through him—a feeling that had only grown stronger in the years since they'd met at university, their relationship developing with a sweet genuineness that they'd taken slowly and carefully.

She looked up as he approached the table, her face lighting up with a smile that momentarily pushed all thoughts of escaped criminals from his mind.

'Sorry I'm a bit late,' he said, leaning down to kiss her before taking the seat opposite.

'You're actually right on time,' Layla replied, tucking her phone away. 'I was early. Got off my admin shift sooner than expected—quiet afternoon at the Trust for once.'

Simon grinned. 'How's work going?'

'The usual healthcare chaos. Filing paperwork that no one will ever read, scheduling appointments that doctors will inevitably reschedule.' She reached for her water glass. 'But enough about NHS bureaucracy. How was your day?'

'Quiet. Found some security holes for Henderson Financial. Fixed them. Documented everything.' Simon shrugged. 'Nothing too exciting, yet.'

'Mmm, protecting the capitalist elite from hackers. Very heroic,' Layla teased, her eyes sparkling. 'Speaking of heroic, did you see the news about that prison break? The Guardian must be concerned.'

Simon kept his expression neutral despite the sudden acceleration of his pulse. 'Why do you say that?'

'Those were his captures, weren't they? The gang that tried to rob the orphanage.' She leaned forward slightly. 'I've noticed you always get interested whenever he's in the news.'

'Do I?'

'Don't play dumb, Simon Jones. We've been together long enough for me to notice your patterns.' Her tone was light, but her eyes held a question. 'Sometimes I think you know more about the Guardian than you let on.'

Simon took a sip of water, using the moment to compose his thoughts. He'd been planning this conversation for weeks now—rehearsing it, preparing for every possible reaction. But now that the moment was here, the carefully considered words seemed to evaporate.

'Maybe I do,' he admitted quietly.

Something in his tone made Layla's expression shift from playful to serious. 'Simon? What are you—'

The waiter arrived to take their order—lamb shish for him, iskender kebab for her—and when they were alone again, Layla reached across the table to take his hand.

'You were about to tell me something,' she prompted gently.

Simon looked at their intertwined fingers, at the silver band on his right hand—its surface etched with ancient runes that only he could see clearly. The weight of his secret pressed against his chest. After months of deliberation, countless conversations with the Ring, he'd decided that Layla deserved to know the truth. Not just deserved it—he wanted her to know. Needed her to understand this fundamental part of his life.

'I've been wanting to talk to you about something important,' he began. 'Something that's a big part of who I am, but that I've kept hidden.'

Layla's gaze was steady, patient. 'Okay.'

'It's not easy to explain, and it'll sound impossible at first, but I promise it's—'

A sudden, intense sensation coursed through Simon's body, emanating from the Ring. It wasn't pain exactly, more like an acute awareness, as if every cell in his body had simultaneously been placed on high alert. Shrill screaming ringing in his ears. His vision blurred momentarily as the Ring pulsed on his finger.

Simon, the Ring's voice was urgent in his mind. *Something is wrong.*

What is it? Simon thought back, keeping his expression as neutral as possible despite the alarm surging through him.

A disturbance in the air, the Ring responded. *Like a calling. Something is happening. Something looming.*

The sensation reminded him of that day years ago when he'd faced Viktor Nemesis—the Ring had vibrated with a similar warning then. But this was different somehow. More like the strange feeling he'd experienced on the skyscraper, that inexplicable sense that the sky was about to fall. Except now, the feeling was amplified tenfold.

'Simon?' Layla's concerned voice pulled him back to the present. 'Are you alright? You look troubled all of a sudden.'

He blinked, focusing on her worried expression. 'I'm fine, just ...' He trailed off, unsure how to explain.

We need to investigate, the Ring insisted. *Now.*

Can it wait? This conversation with Layla is important.

It cannot. This disturbance is unusual, something is off. Someone could be in serious danger. We should investigate.

Simon suppressed a sigh. Of course it would happen now, just as he was finally ready to reveal his secret.

'Layla, I'm sorry, but something's come up. An emergency.' He hated the words even as he spoke them, hated seeing the familiar disappointment cross her face.

'Work emergency on a Friday night?' She withdrew her hand slowly.

'Not work, no.' Simon held her gaze, making a decision. 'It's related to what I was about to tell you. I promise I'll explain everything when I get back—the whole truth. No more secrets.'

Scepticism mingled with concern in her eyes. 'Is everything okay? Are you in some kind of trouble?'

'I'm not in trouble,' he assured her, already standing and dropping enough cash on the table to cover their meals. 'But someone else might be. I wouldn't leave if it wasn't important.'

Layla studied him for a long moment before nodding slowly. 'Go. But I'm holding you to that promise. The whole truth when you get back.'

'The whole truth,' Simon confirmed, leaning down to kiss her quickly. 'I'll call you later.'

As he stepped out into the evening air, the sensation from the Ring intensified—a pulling, urgent feeling directing him eastward.

What exactly are we looking for? Simon asked mentally as he ducked into the first empty alley he found.

I'm not certain, the Ring admitted. *It's a strange disturbance in the air, almost like a calling. Something isn't right.*

Simon closed his eyes, focusing on the connection between himself and the Ring. The silver band seemed to melt and flow, dark purple spreading across his skin like liquid metal, enveloping his body in a symbiotic embrace as the Guardian emerged—his everyday clothes disappearing beneath the transformation.

Then let's go find out what it is.

With a powerful leap, he took to the rooftops, his glowing purple eyes scanning the darkening city as he moved eastward, towards whatever mysterious force had called him away from one of the most important conversations of his life.

CHAPTER 15

Simon moved through the night like a shadow, his enhanced form allowing him to traverse the urban landscape with fluid grace. The strange sensation from the Ring had led him eastward, towards the old industrial estate in East London where abandoned warehouses stood as hollow reminders of the city's manufacturing past. With each passing minute, the disturbance grew stronger, pulling him deeper into the maze of derelict buildings.

It's coming from that structure, the Ring communicated as Simon perched on a rooftop, surveying a particularly dilapidated warehouse. The building's windows were mostly shattered, its metal exterior rusted and peeling, yet something about it seemed ... off. There were no signs of recent activity—no footprints in the dust, no vehicles nearby, no lights visible from within.

I don't like this, Simon thought back, his glowing purple eyes scanning for any movement or heat signatures. *Too quiet.*

Agreed. Proceed with caution.

Simon dropped silently from his vantage point, landing in a crouch beside a loading bay door that hung partially off its track. He slipped through the gap, his form adapting to the tight space, and emerged into the cavernous interior of the warehouse. Moonlight filtered through broken skylights, casting geometric patterns across the concrete floor. Empty shelving units and abandoned equipment created a labyrinth of shadows within the space.

The Guardian moved silently, each step calculated, each shadow analysed for potential threats. Years of experience had taught him to trust his instincts, and right now, every sense was screaming that something wasn't right. Yet the warehouse appeared completely deserted.

The disturbance is stronger here, the Ring noted. *Close.*

Simon navigated through the maze of abandoned machinery, following the Ring's guidance until he reached what must have once been the central work area. The space opened up, the ceiling rising higher above, moonlight streaming down more directly.

And there, hovering approximately three feet off the ground in the centre of the room, was a small circular device no larger than a dinner plate. It emitted no visible light, but Simon could feel it—a low-frequency vibration that seemed to resonate directly with the Ring, accompanied by what felt like a shrill screaming in his ears, similar to the sensation he experienced when someone was in imminent danger. The sound wasn't physical, but something only he could perceive, setting his nerves on edge.

What is that? he wondered, approaching slowly, maintaining his distance.

Unknown, the Ring replied. *But it's the source of the disturbance. It's ... calling to us somehow. And that screaming sensation—it's designed to trigger our protective instincts.*

Simon circled the device cautiously, examining it from all angles without touching it. Its surface was smooth, metallic, with intricate patterns etched into its circumference—patterns that reminded him vaguely of the runes on his Ring, yet distinctly different. More alien.

I can feel it, Simon communicated. *Like it's emitting a frequency only we can detect.*

He took another step closer, his curiosity momentarily overriding his caution. The device continued to hover, rotating slowly in place, seemingly innocuous despite the strange vibrations it emitted.

It happened in an instant. The Ring's energy spiked sharply, a warning flaring through Simon's consciousness. *MOVE!*

Pure instinct took over. Simon backflipped away from the device just as a blinding arc of electricity crackled through the space where he had stood a split second before. The bolt struck the concrete floor, sending fragments of stone exploding outward.

He landed in a defensive crouch, only to feel a tremendous impact against his back that sent him staggering forward. Before he could regain his balance, something sharp and metallic struck his shoulder—a blade-like projectile that embedded itself momentarily before he could dislodge it.

Pain blossomed from the wound, but Simon had no time to assess the damage. A visible distortion in the air—like a heat wave but more concentrated—raced towards him. He attempted to dodge, but the shockwave caught him squarely in the chest, lifting him off his feet and hurling him backwards with incredible force.

His body crashed through a concrete support column before slamming into the far wall, the impact sending cracks spiderwebbing outward. Dust and debris rained down as Simon slid to the floor, momentarily stunned by the coordinated assault.

Simon! The Ring's voice cut through the momentary disorientation. *Multiple attackers. We need to move!*

Simon pushed himself upright, ignoring the pain radiating from his shoulder and back. His enhanced physiology was already working to heal the damage, but he knew he needed to reposition, to get his bearings.

'I told you he'd show up.' A familiar voice echoed through the warehouse, followed by a deep chuckle. 'The do-gooder couldn't help himself.'

Four figures emerged from different positions around the warehouse, stepping into the moonlight streaming from above. Each wore what looked to be advanced technology, unlike anything Simon had seen before. Yet, beneath these enhancements, he recognised their faces immediately.

The man in the front—Dushane Barracks—now wore gauntlets and a chest piece covered in intricate circuitry that pulsed with energy. 'Remember us, Guardian? We certainly remember you.'

'Impossible,' Simon muttered, his mind racing. 'Though I did see the news. How'd you get out of Belmarsh?'

'Wouldn't you love to know,' replied Wei Zhang, descending slowly from above, a sleek harness with sharp-edged metallic wings allowing him to hover effortlessly. 'Amazing what technology can accomplish these days.'

Mateo Reyes stepped forward next, his massive frame now encased in an exoskeleton that made him tower over the others, his footsteps leaving small craters in the concrete floor. 'We've been upgraded.'

The fourth figure—Callum Briggs—moved to complete their semicircle around Simon, electricity crackling around his hands as he flexed his fingers within what appeared to be specialized gloves connected to a full-body suit laced with conductive material.

'Just as the alien said,' Dushane continued, a cruel smile spreading across his face. 'You couldn't resist the call.'

'Alien?' Simon questioned, trying to buy time as his body continued healing. 'What are you talking about?'

Wei gestured towards the hovering device that had initially drawn Simon to the warehouse. 'Our benefactor was quite specific about this little creation. Said it emits a frequency that only those with six or more senses could detect.' His eyes narrowed as he studied Simon's reaction. 'He was right again. You're definitely not normal, are you, Guardian?'

'You have no idea what you're dealing with,' Simon warned, rising to his full height despite the pain still radiating from his wounds.

'No,' Dushane countered, his gauntlets beginning to glow with building energy. 'It's you who has no idea. We're not the same men you humiliated before. We're something else now.'

The four spread out in a tactical formation that Simon recognised immediately as professional and practiced. This was definitely an upgrade. They had been trained, equipped, and prepared specifically for this encounter.

'We are the Reclaimers,' Dushane declared, raising his gauntlets. 'I'm Shockwave.'

'Skyfang,' Wei added, his wings extending to their full impressive span.

'Titan,' rumbled Mateo, the exoskeleton whirring as he clenched massive metal fists.

'Volt,' Callum finished, electricity dancing between his fingertips.

Simon's mind raced, assessing his options. Four enhanced opponents, each with lethal technology he'd never faced before, in a confined space with limited escape routes. The trap had been expertly laid, and he'd walked right into it.

'And we've come to collect what you stole from us,' Shockwave finished, his voice hardening. 'Starting with your dignity.'

The Guardian shifted into a defensive stance, the Ring's energy flowing through him, preparing for the inevitable assault. The Reclaimers had caught him by surprise once—it wouldn't happen again.

'Then come and try,' he challenged, his glowing purple eyes fixed on his opponents.

Four against one. Not the best odds, but Simon had faced worse.

Hadn't he?

Chapter 16

Simon had seconds to assess the situation as the Reclaimers closed in on him. The warehouse offered limited cover and multiple hazards—exposed support beams, debris, rusted machinery. His shoulder throbbed where Skyfang's blade had struck, but the Ring was already working to accelerate his healing.

They're coordinated, the Ring observed. *And their equipment is unlike anything we've encountered on Earth.*

So we adapt, Simon replied mentally as he shifted into a defensive stance.

Shockwave moved first, raising his gauntlets and unleashing a concentrated blast of concussive force. Simon leapt sideways, narrowly avoiding the impact as it demolished a concrete pillar behind him. Before he could fully recover, Volt sent a crackling arc of electricity surging across the floor towards him.

The current caught Simon's leg, sending a numbing sensation up his body. It wasn't intensely painful, but the momentary paralysis was enough to leave him vulnerable as Titan charged, his exoskeleton whirring with mechanical power.

Simon twisted to avoid the brunt of the impact, but Titan's enhanced strength still sent him flying backwards. He managed to control his trajectory, rebounding off a wall and launching himself towards the scaffolding above—only to find Skyfang already there, wings extended, launching a barrage of razor-sharp projectiles.

Simon raised his arm, allowing the Ring to form a partial shield that deflected most of the blades. One sliced across his cheek, another grazed his ribs—stinging but superficial wounds. He dropped back to the ground, immediately having to dodge another shockwave blast that caught the edge of his shoulder, spinning him violently.

'Not so confident now, are you?' Dushane taunted, his gauntlets recharging with a high-pitched whine. 'Four of us. One of you. And we know exactly what you're capable of.'

Do they? the Ring questioned, a hint of defiance in its mental voice.

Simon used the momentary exchange to analyse the patterns emerging. The Reclaimers were fighting as a unit, covering each other's blind spots, but their coordination still showed signs of being recently developed. There were gaps—milliseconds where their attacks didn't overlap perfectly.

And more importantly, beneath the advanced technology, they were still human.

As Volt unleashed another electrical barrage, Simon didn't dodge this time. He let the current hit him directly, enduring the temporary discomfort as the Ring adapted to the frequency. The electricity coursed through him, making his muscles spasm briefly, but the sensation was already less debilitating than the first strike.

Their pattern, Simon communicated to the Ring. *Volt stuns. Titan hits. Skyfang prevents aerial escape. Shockwave delivers the heavy damage.*

Break the pattern, the Ring suggested.

Simon charged directly at Volt—the opposite of what the Reclaimers would expect. Callum's eyes widened behind his mask as he fired another electrical blast, but Simon was ready this time. The Ring channelled the current, not completely neutralizing it but diminishing its paralyzing effect.

Before Volt could retreat, Simon caught him with a sweeping leg strike that sent him crashing into a stack of empty crates. One threat temporarily neutralized.

Titan roared as he rushed forward, mechanical servos whining as the exoskeleton amplified his already impressive strength. Simon didn't try to match the brute force—instead, he used Titan's momentum against him, redirecting his charge with a precise strike to the exoskeleton's joint mechanism.

Mateo stumbled but recovered quickly, spinning to face Simon again. 'You'll need to hit harder than that,' he growled, swinging a massive armoured fist.

Simon dodged the blow, studying the suit's movements. 'Impressive tech,' he said, voice calm despite the intensity of the fight. 'But there's always a weakness.'

A shockwave blast caught Simon in the back, sending him sprawling forward directly into Titan's waiting grasp.

The armoured hands clamped around his throat, lifting him off the ground.

'Got you,' Mateo grinned, squeezing tighter.

Simon felt the pressure building, his vision beginning to blur at the edges. Above, Skyfang circled like a predatory bird, ready to strike if he broke free. Behind Titan, Shockwave was preparing another blast, this one potentially lethal at such close range.

Inside Simon, something dark and primal stirred—the full power of the Ring, tempting him to release it completely. To stop holding back. To show these humans what real power looked like. The urge was intoxicating, promising swift victory if he'd only surrender to it.

Simon, the Ring cautioned, sensing his thoughts. *Remember the balance.*

With a tremendous effort of will, Simon reined in the darker impulses. He didn't need to release his full power to win this fight. He just needed to be smarter.

His eyes flashed brighter as he focused on Titan's exoskeleton, his enhanced vision allowing him to spot what he was looking for—the power distribution node at the base of the spine. With a swift kick, Simon struck the vulnerable spot. The exoskeleton shuddered, its grip momentarily loosening.

That split second was all Simon needed. He broke free, simultaneously pushing off Titan's chest with enough force to send the armoured man staggering backwards—directly into the path of Shockwave's blast.

The concussive force meant for Simon hit Titan instead, the impact amplified by the metal of the exoskeleton. Mateo crashed through a wall, disappearing in a cloud of debris and dust.

'Mateo!' Shockwave shouted, his composure cracking for the first time.

'Two down,' Simon said, rising to his full height. 'Who's next?'

Skyfang swooped down from above, his wings' razor edges whistling through the air. Simon waited until the last possible moment before sidestepping, grabbing one of the extended wings as it passed. The metal cut into his palm, but the Ring quickly formed a protective layer that allowed him to maintain his grip.

With a powerful twist, Simon used Wei's momentum against him, slamming him into a support column. The impact dented the gravity harness, causing it to sputter and spark. Skyfang managed to stay airborne, but his flight pattern became erratic, one wing no longer responding properly.

'You're fighting the inevitable,' Wei called, trying to regain altitude. 'We've been enhanced specifically to defeat you!'

'Enhancement isn't experience,' Simon replied, tracking Skyfang's compromised flight pattern. 'And technology isn't power.'

From the corner of his eye, Simon spotted Volt recovering, electricity once again building around his hands. Simultaneously, Shockwave was moving to a better firing position, his gauntlets fully recharged. They were attempting to catch him in a crossfire.

Simon waited for Volt to fire first. As the electrical blast arced towards him, he leapt into its path—but instead of trying to dodge, he positioned himself to redirect it. The Ring caught the current, channelling it through Simon's body and out through his extended hand—directly at the now-descending Skyfang.

The electricity struck Wei's damaged harness, causing a cascade of failures. Sparks erupted from the control systems as the gravity mechanism failed completely. Skyfang plummeted, crashing into a pile of rusted machinery with a sickening crunch of metal on metal.

'Wei!' Volt cried out, his attention momentarily diverted.

That momentary distraction was all Simon needed. He closed the distance between them in a blur of motion, delivering a cross punch to the junction of Volt's suit where the power regulator was located. The blow wasn't particularly strong, but it didn't need to be—the disruption to the electrical systems caused a feedback loop that sent Callum convulsing to the floor, his own suit temporarily overloading his nervous system.

'Just you and me now,' Simon said, turning to face Shockwave.

A roar of rage interrupted as Titan emerged from the debris, his exoskeleton dented and sparking but still functioning. He charged at Simon from behind, mechanical limbs propelling him forward with renewed fury.

'I'm not done with you yet!' Mateo bellowed.

Simon turned calmly, bracing himself as Titan's bulldozing force collided with him. The impact would have sent any normal person flying, but Simon simply planted his feet, absorbing the tremendous force. His body barely moved despite Titan's exoskeleton whining at maximum output, servos screaming as they pushed forward.

'Not possible,' Mateo gasped, disbelief evident in his voice as his technologically-enhanced strength failed to budge the Guardian.

'My turn,' Simon replied simply. In one smooth motion, he sidestepped, pivoted, and seized Titan's right arm. Using the enemy's momentum like a judo master, he twisted low and powerslammed him over his shoulder. Titan's heavy frame crashed into the ground with a seismic thud, dust and debris erupting from the floor.

Before the armoured man could react, Simon hoisted him up for the final combo. His knee shot upward with devastating precision, striking a junction point in his suit. Titan barely recovered as Simon's fist connected with his armoured chest—a focused blow that sent Mateo flying backwards, his armoured form crashing once again through debris before coming to rest, the exoskeleton finally powered down completely.

Simon turned back to Dushane, who had witnessed the display with growing apprehension.

'Now, as I was saying,' Simon continued as if there had been no interruption, 'it's just you and me.'

Dushane's expression darkened as he raised both gauntlets. 'I don't need them to finish you.'

The warehouse filled with a deafening roar as Shockwave unleashed his most powerful blast yet. The air itself seemed to distort as the concussive force ripped towards Simon, tearing up the concrete floor in its path.

Simon didn't dodge this time. Instead, he braced himself, allowing his suit to harden and adapt, forming a protective shield around him. The impact was tremendous, driving him backwards, his feet leaving deep furrows in the concrete as he fought to maintain his position. Pain lanced through his body as the protective layer absorbed the worst of the blast but couldn't negate it completely.

When the roar finally subsided, Simon remained standing, though visibly battered. His breath came in short gasps, but his glowing eyes remained fixed on Shockwave.

'Impressive,' Dushane admitted, a hint of genuine respect in his voice. 'But how many more of those can you take?'

Simon didn't bother to answer. Instead, he shot forward with startling speed, closing the distance before Dushane could charge another powerful blast. Shockwave tried to fire a hasty, weaker shot, but Simon was already weaving past it, his movement a blur as he advanced relentlessly.

Dushane's confidence crumbled as Simon reached him, fear flickering across his face as he realized his most devastating weapon couldn't stop the Guardian's approach. He fired rapidly now, desperation replacing tactical accuracy, but Simon slipped between the blasts with fluid grace.

'Stay back!' he shouted, his voice cracking slightly as Simon reached striking distance.

Simon moved like water between the blasts, each step bringing him closer until he was within striking distance. Dushane attempted to deliver a point-blank blast, but

Simon caught his wrist, twisting until the gauntlet was aimed away from both of them.

'Your technology is impressive,' Simon said, his voice calm despite the intensity of their struggle. 'But it's only as good as the person using it.'

With his free hand, Simon delivered a hard uppercut to Dushane's stomach—not enough to seriously injure, but sufficient to knock the wind from his lungs. As Shockwave gasped for breath, Simon disabled the gauntlets, crushing key components beyond repair.

Around them, the other Reclaimers were stirring, Titan trying to force his damaged exoskeleton to move, Volt slowly regaining control of his limbs, Skyfang weakly attempting to disentangle himself from the wreckage where he'd fallen.

But their leader remained in Simon's grip, defeated.

With a swift movement, Simon pinned Dushane against a wall, purple eyes blazing with controlled fury as he held him suspended several inches off the ground. The fight had taken its toll—Simon's body was bruised and bleeding in a couple places—but the dark rage that had tempted him earlier had been channelled into a cold, focused determination.

'Now,' Simon said, his voice dropping to a dangerous whisper, 'you're going to tell me everything. Starting with this "alien" you mentioned. Who is he? What does he want? And why did he help you?'

***

Dushane's eyes widened as he realized that for all the physical punishment of the battle, the true ordeal was only just beginning. The Guardian wasn't just a physical force to be reckoned with—he was an intelligence gathering information. And in that moment, despite all his technological enhancements, Dushane felt truly vulnerable under that piercing purple gaze.

CHAPTER 17

Dushane had never considered himself a man who scared easily. He'd faced down rival gang leaders, corrupt police officers, and hardened killers without so much as a tremor in his voice. He'd built his reputation on strategic brilliance and unflinching resolve. But dangling several inches off the ground, held by a single hand against the crumbling warehouse wall, looking into those glowing purple eyes—Dushane felt something he hadn't experienced since childhood.

Pure, primal fear.

Up close, the Guardian's aura was unmistakably charged with energy, like the heaviness before a lightning storm. And those eyes ... they didn't just glow. They seemed to see through skin, through bone, down to the core of what made Dushane himself.

He struggled to maintain his composure, refusing to give the vigilante the satisfaction of seeing him break. Around them, the warehouse was eerily quiet except for the occasional groan from his fallen teammates. Their grand plan, their technological advantages, their careful preparations—all rendered meaningless in minutes.

'The alien,' the Guardian repeated, his voice unnaturally calm given the violence that had preceded this moment. 'Who is he?'

Dushane forced a smirk. 'Who says there is one?'

The pressure against his throat increased slightly—not enough to cut off his air entirely, but sufficient to make breathing uncomfortable. The message was clear: this wasn't a negotiation.

'Don't waste my time,' the Guardian said. 'Your equipment isn't Earth technology. The device that lured me here operates on ultra advanced principles, something none of you could have engineered. Someone helped you. Someone who wanted to draw me out.'

Dushane weighed his options quickly. Eradax had warned them that if captured, they should reveal only limited information—enough to intrigue the Guardian, but not enough to expose the full scope of their benefactor's plans. The alien had been confident that even if they failed in their first confrontation, the data collected would prove valuable.

'His name is Eradax,' Dushane finally answered, seeing no advantage in withholding that much. 'Calls himself the Collector of Relics.'

The Guardian's expression didn't change, but Dushane felt a subtle shift in the energy surrounding him—a ripple of recognition, perhaps, or concern.

'What does he want?'

Dushane attempted a casual shrug despite his precarious position. 'Not big on sharing his grand plans with the help, is he? But he's got a particular interest in you. Or more specifically, in something you possess.'

The Guardian's free hand moved with startling speed, catching Dushane's right wrist and twisting it to an angle just short of breaking. Pain shot up his arm, sharp and immediate.

'Be specific,' the Guardian demanded, his voice dead serious.

Dushane's composure slipped a fraction, a hiss of pain escaping through clenched teeth. 'Some kind of relic you possess,' he gasped. 'He wasn't big on details. Just said you have something of immense value to him. Worth crossing galaxies for, apparently.'

The Guardian's gaze intensified, though his expression remained unreadable.

'How did he find you?' The Guardian's question pulled Dushane back to the present situation.

'Prison break wasn't our doing. Systems failed, doors opened. Next thing we know, we're being offered tech beyond our wildest dreams in exchange for testing your abilities.' Dushane managed a thin smile. 'Simple business transaction.'

'And you didn't question why an alien would help four criminals escape prison just to fight me?'

Dushane gave a short laugh. 'Question the man offering you the keys to the kingdom? That's bad business. Besides, I enjoyed taking a crack at you. My only regret—I didn't get to finish you.'

The Guardian's expression hardened. 'Where is he now?'

'No idea,' Dushane lied smoothly. 'He contacts us. Not the other way around. Some sort of advanced communication device. Says when he needs us, he'll find us.'

The vigilante studied him intently, those unnatural eyes seeming to peer directly into Dushane's thoughts. After a long moment, the Guardian released his wrist, though he maintained his grip on Dushane's collar, keeping him pinned against the wall.

'What else did he tell you about this relic?'

Dushane recognized an opportunity to regain some control of the conversation. The Guardian's interest in Eradax's knowledge was clear—perhaps this was a vulnerability he could exploit.

'Not much. That it's powerful. That you shouldn't have it.' Dushane paused, watching for reactions. 'That it wasn't meant for someone like you.'

A flicker of something—doubt? anger?—passed across the Guardian's face. Good. Dushane had struck a nerve.

'And you believed everything an alien told you?' the Guardian asked, his tone deceptively casual.

'I believe the results,' Dushane replied, glancing meaningfully at the advanced gauntlets on his wrists, now damaged beyond repair. 'Man delivers what he promises. Good business.'

The Guardian fell silent, seemingly processing this new information. Dushane used the moment to assess his situation. Wei was unconscious, buried under machinery. Mateo's exoskeleton had completely powered down, rendering him immobile. Callum was still twitching occasionally from the electrical feedback. No help would come from his team.

His only advantage now was psychological—finding the right words to destabilize the Guardian's confidence. And suddenly, Dushane remembered something that might work.

'You know,' he began, his voice taking on a conversational tone despite the pain in his wrist, 'I did some research on you after our first encounter. Found an interesting article from a few years back. Early days of the Guardian's appearances.'

The vigilante's attention returned fully to Dushane, his eyes narrowing slightly.

'Mysterious deaths connected to the Guardian's activities. Including a crime boss ... what was his name?' Dushane pretended to search his memory. 'Marcus Crawford, wasn't it? Found with his insides leaking out.'

The air around them seemed to grow colder as the Guardian's energy shifted subtly. Dushane knew he'd hit his mark.

'What happened since then?' Dushane continued, pushing his advantage. 'Get squeamish? Decide you didn't like all the blood?' His lips curled into a sneer. 'Coward.'

The Guardian remained perfectly still, which somehow was more terrifying than any visible reaction.

'You know what I'm going to do when I get out?' Dushane pressed on, recklessness born of desperation giving him courage. 'I'm going to find out who you really are. And then I'm going to find anyone you care about. And

I'll kill them. For free.' He emphasized the last words with particular venom. 'Just to watch you break.'

For three heartbeats, nothing happened. Then the Guardian moved.

The first blow caught Dushane in the solar plexus, driving the air from his lungs in a painful rush. The second struck his ribs with a punishing blow—enough to crack but not break them. The third was an open-handed strike to his shoulder that sent white-hot pain lancing down his arm as the joint dislocated with a sickening pop.

Through it all, Dushane noted with horrified fascination that the Guardian's expression never changed. There was no rage, no satisfaction—just the mechanical precision of someone performing a necessary task. Somehow, that controlled violence was far more terrifying than any emotional outburst.

'The doctors will be able to fix that,' the Guardian said, nodding towards Dushane's dislocated shoulder. 'Eventually. But you'll remember the pain every time you reach for something.' He leaned closer, his voice dropping to a whisper. 'And you'll remember this: if you ever threaten anyone else again, I won't stop at a shoulder.'

Dushane tried to respond with defiance, but the pain made it difficult to form words. The Guardian released his grip, allowing Dushane to slide down the wall to a sitting position.

'Your alien friend used you,' the Guardian continued, standing over him now. 'You were just data points to him. A test. And now that test is over.'

Dushane managed to find his voice, though it emerged as little more than a rasp. 'This isn't over. The Reclaimers aren't finished with you.'

'The Reclaimers are going back to prison,' the Guardian replied. 'And I'm going to have a conversation with your benefactor.'

As Dushane opened his mouth for one final act of defiance, the Guardian's fist connected with his jaw, plunging him into unconsciousness. The last thing Dushane saw were those glowing purple eyes, impassive and inhuman, watching him fall.

Then nothing at all.

CHAPTER 18

Simon watched as Dushane slumped unconscious against the wall, the criminal's face already beginning to swell where his fist had connected. The warehouse fell silent except for the occasional groan from the other Reclaimers and the distant sound of settling debris. The confrontation had lasted less than fifteen minutes, but the implications of what he'd learned would echo far longer.

They were bait, the Ring observed in his mind. *Used to draw us out.*

And we took it, Simon replied, surveying the defeated criminals. Another few arch enemies made, and they all had sworn personal vendettas against him. The Guardian had faced organized crime before, but never opponents with such advanced technology like this.

Eradax, Simon thought, tasting the alien's name. *The Collector of Relics.*

It's been a long time since anyone has sought me across the stars, the Ring responded, its mental voice thoughtful. *Whoever this being is, he possesses knowledge and technology far beyond Earth's current capabilities.*

Simon moved methodically around the warehouse, gathering pieces of the criminals' damaged equipment. He examined Wei's gravity harness with particular interest, noting the alien inscriptions etched into its control nodes. The technology was sleek but sturdy, designed for combat rather than mere aesthetics.

Humans definitely couldn't have built this, could they? he asked the Ring as he studied the intricate mechanisms.

No, came the confident reply. *The principles at work here are thousands of years ahead of current Earth science. The gravitational manipulation alone would require understanding of spatial mechanics that your scientists have barely theorized.*

Simon nodded silently, then methodically began to disable each piece of equipment. He damaged Volt's conductive gloves, warped the articulation joints of Skyfang's wings, and struck the power regulator of Titan's exoskeleton until it cracked and sparked. When he reached Shockwave's gauntlets, he removed the primary energy cells, rendering them inert.

Thorough, the Ring observed.

Necessary, Simon replied. *Technology like this doesn't belong in anyone's hands—especially not theirs.*

Satisfied that the gear was unusable, Simon moved to secure the Reclaimers. Finding a storage room with industrial supplies, he retrieved several lengths of heavy chain. One by one, he bound the unconscious criminals, ensuring that Titan's damaged exoskeleton was completely immobilized and that the remnants of Volt's equipment were placed far from reach.

When he reached Dushane, Simon paused, looking down at the man who had threatened to kill anyone close to him. Marcus Crawford's name echoed in his mind—a reminder of darker days, before he had fully understood the responsibility that came with the Ring's power. Before balance and restraint had become his guiding principles.

He was trying to provoke you, the Ring noted.

It almost worked, Simon admitted, securing Dushane's hands with particular care.

As he finished restraining the last of the Reclaimers, Simon's enhanced hearing picked up the distant wail of police sirens. Someone had reported the battle—not surprising given the multiple shockwave blasts that had shattered windows and damaged support structures.

Time to go, he thought, gathering the pieces of the lure device that had drawn him here.

What about them? the Ring asked, referring to the defeated criminals.

Simon surveyed the scene one last time. *The police can handle them now. I've disabled their equipment beyond quick repair. And we have what we came for.*

He pocketed the alien device, ensuring it was completely powered down. Its strange frequency no longer called to him, but the technology itself might provide clues about this mysterious collector from beyond Earth.

The sirens grew louder as Simon made his way to the roof. Through a broken skylight, he could see police vehicles converging on the warehouse, their blue lights painting the surrounding buildings in rhythmic flashes. He remained in the shadows, watching as armed officers approached the building with caution.

We should inform the authorities about the alien threat, the Ring suggested.

Simon shook his head slightly. *And tell them what? That an extraterrestrial collector is hunting for magical artefacts? They'd think it was a hoax or, worse, they'd believe it and panic. We handle this ourselves—for now.*

As the police breached the warehouse entrance below, Simon slipped away across the rooftops, moving silently through the London night. The physical exertion was automatic, allowing his mind to process everything he'd learned.

An alien called Eradax was on Earth, searching for the Ring. He had technology advanced enough to break four criminals out of a maximum-security prison, enhance them with weaponry beyond human capability, and create a device that could specifically target his Ring through a unique frequency. This wasn't a random encounter or opportunistic theft—this was a calculated hunt by someone who knew exactly what they were looking for.

What would a collector want with you? Simon asked the Ring as he paused on a water tower, overlooking the city lights.

I am not the first Fallen Ring, it responded. *There are others, as you know, scattered throughout the cosmos. Some dormant, some bonded. All powerful. To one who collects rare artefacts, we would be prized acquisitions.*

Can he take you from me? The question had been lingering at the edge of Simon's thoughts since Dushane had first mentioned the alien.

The Ring was silent for a moment before answering. *Not easily. Our bond is strong, forged through years of harmony. But I cannot say it's impossible. If his knowledge and technology are as advanced as they appear…*

Simon felt a chill that had nothing to do with the night air. The Ring had become more than a tool or weapon to him—it was a partner, a constant companion through the darkest moments of his life. The thought of losing it to some cosmic collector was unacceptable.

His mind turned to Layla, waiting at the restaurant he had left so abruptly. He had promised her the whole truth when he returned. Now that truth had become even more complicated and dangerous. If Eradax was willing to arm criminals and set traps, what other methods might he employ to get what he wanted? Would he target those close to Simon if he discovered his identity?

I need to warn her, Simon thought. *And we need to find this collector before he finds us.*

He took a running leap to the next building, the Ring's power flowing through him as he soared through the night air. Question after question tumbled through his mind: How had Eradax tracked the Ring to Earth? What were his true capabilities? Was he working alone, or were there others? And most urgently—where was he now?

The answers wouldn't come easily, but Simon was certain of one thing: the Reclaimers had been just the opening move in a much larger game. A test, as he had told Dushane. And the real challenge was still to come.

As he bounded across the London rooftops, Simon felt the weight of this new threat settling onto his shoulders. No longer was he simply the Guardian of London, protecting the city from human criminals and opportunistic villains. Now he stood as Earth's unwitting defender against a threat from beyond the stars—a collector who had crossed galaxies for the power encircling his very finger.

The hunt had begun. But who, exactly, was the hunter, and who was the prey? That remained to be seen.

CHAPTER 19

T he night air whistled past Simon as he bounded across the city skyline, each leap carrying him closer to Layla and the difficult conversation that awaited. His mind raced with questions about Eradax and the implications of an alien collector hunting for his Ring. The battle with the Reclaimers had been exhausting, both physically and mentally, yet the night was far from over.

His body was still in the process of healing—the Ring's power accelerating his recovery, but the wounds from Shockwave's concussive blasts and Skyfang's stinging blades had taken their toll. Simon winced as he landed on a rooftop, feeling the strain in his still-mending muscles.

We should consider informing the authorities, the Ring suggested again as Simon paused atop a water tower, momentarily catching his breath.

And tell them what? Simon countered, scanning the cityscape. *That an alien is after magical jewellery? We'd be labelled as either crazy or a threat.*

Simon's gaze settled on a secluded route across several abandoned buildings that would lead him towards Layla's house. The path would take longer but offered privacy—a chance to gather his thoughts before facing Layla.

At minimum, we should warn Layla. And your family, the Ring insisted. *If this collector is as determined as he seems—*

Simon's enhanced senses flared with sudden warning. The air around him shifted imperceptibly—a subtle distortion that ordinary humans would never notice. Instinctively, he dropped into a defensive stance, eyes scanning for the source of the disturbance.

Behind— the Ring began, but the warning came too late.

Something struck Simon with tremendous force, sending him flying from his perch. He twisted mid-air, managing to land in a controlled roll on a lower rooftop. As he regained his footing, the air before him rippled like heat waves above hot asphalt, and a figure stepped through what appeared to be an invisible doorway.

The being that appeared was unlike anything Simon had ever encountered. Standing nearly eight feet tall, its body appeared to be composed of some metallic alloy with a rigid, armoured exterior. Its eyes glowed crimson in a face that seemed both mechanical and organic, with sharp, angular features that were vaguely humanoid yet unmistakably alien.

'At last,' the entity said, its voice resonating with an otherworldly timbre. 'The Ring-bearer reveals himself.'

Simon maintained his defensive stance, his mind racing to process this new threat. 'Eradax, I presume.'

A sound emanated from the alien that might have been laughter. 'My reputation precedes me. Good. That will make this more efficient.' He gestured towards Simon's hand. 'You possess something that doesn't belong to you.'

'I think the Ring disagrees,' Simon replied, keeping his distance. Through their bond, he could feel the Ring's energy surging, responding to the immediate danger.

Eradax tilted his head, studying Simon with those unnerving crimson eyes. 'You speak as if it has consciousness. Interesting. The symbiosis is more advanced than I anticipated.'

Without warning, Eradax's right arm transformed, the metallic surface flowing and reshaping into what appeared to be a cannon. Before Simon could react, a blast of energy erupted from the weapon, striking him squarely in the chest.

The impact sent Simon crashing through the roof access door behind him. Pain radiated through his body as he struggled to regain his footing among the debris. The Ring's protection had absorbed much of the blast, but not all of it.

He's fast, the Ring communicated. *And his weapons are formidable.*

Tell me something I don't know, Simon thought back, rolling sideways as Eradax fired again, the energy blast obliterating the concrete where he had been standing moments before.

'Your evasive capabilities are impressive,' Eradax remarked, stepping forward. 'But ultimately futile.'

Simon launched himself at the alien, moving with enhanced speed that had caught countless opponents off guard. But Eradax seemed to anticipate the attack, his left arm transforming into a blade that slashed across Simon's midsection as they collided.

The Ring's protective covering absorbed most of the damage, but Simon felt the underlying sting as the blade's edge penetrated deeper than expected. He countered with a series of strikes aimed at what appeared to be the alien's joints. His blows connected with impact, denting and damaging Eradax's metallic form, but the alien barely reacted—the damage minimal compared to what such strikes would do to any Earth-based opponent.

'Primitive combat techniques,' Eradax observed, his tone almost disappointed as he withstood the damage Simon had inflicted. 'Is this how you defeated my test subjects? Brute force and simple evasion?'

Simon didn't respond, focusing instead on finding a vulnerability in the alien's defences. He feinted left, then delivered a powerful roundhouse kick that connected solidly with Eradax's head. The impact was significant, actually knocking the alien backwards and leaving a visible dent in his metallic skull.

For a moment, victory seemed possible. Then Eradax steadied himself, the significant dent in his head remaining as he assessed Simon with renewed interest. What would have incapacitated or killed any human opponent had only managed to catch the alien collector's attention.

'Better,' the alien said, genuine appreciation in his voice despite the damage to his metallic skull. 'You do possess remarkable strength. The damage will require repair aboard my vessel later. But it changes nothing about our current situation.'

With frightening speed, Eradax closed the distance between them. This time his hand transformed into something resembling a hammer, the impact catching Simon's shoulder with enough force to send him crashing through the wall and onto an adjacent rooftop.

The collision disrupted the Ring's protective covering, causing it to momentarily retract in places. Simon felt cool air against his exposed cheek and saw the sleeve of his ordinary clothing beneath, partially revealed before the Ring's protection flowed back to cover him completely.

Eradax emerged from the hole in the wall, his crimson gaze fixed on Simon with new interest. 'A human,' he said, though his tone suggested this wasn't a revelation. 'And young, too. How curious that a Fallen Ring would bond with such a basic species. You must possess some quality I cannot perceive.'

Simon pushed himself to his feet, ignoring the pain radiating from his shoulder. 'Maybe it just doesn't like collectors who treat sentient artefacts like trophies.'

'The Ring is not sentient in the way you understand,' Eradax replied, stepping closer. 'It is power, ancient and extraordinary, but it is a tool—one that was never meant for human hands.'

'Yet here we are,' Simon countered, preparing for another attack.

Eradax paused, studying him with clinical detachment. 'Simon Jones,' he said, the use of his real name hitting

Simon like a physical blow. 'Systems analyst at Sentinel Cybersecurity. Formerly a university student. Son of Sarah Jones.'

Cold dread washed over Simon. 'How—'

'Your face was visible for one point seven seconds,' Eradax explained matter-of-factly. 'Sufficient time for facial recognition against the monitoring systems I've accessed. Your identity was already among my higher probability candidates based on movement patterns and temporal analysis.'

He took another step forward. 'And Layla Thompson. Administrative assistant at a North London NHS Trust. Someone you seem to care about quite a lot.'

Rage boiled up inside Simon, the Ring's energy responding to his emotional state, pulsing with dangerous potential. 'If you go near her—'

'That depends entirely on you,' Eradax interrupted, his voice eerily calm. 'I offer you a choice, Simon Jones. Surrender the Ring willingly, and your associations remain undisturbed. Resist, and I will be forced to employ alternative methods of acquisition.'

The alien's right hand transformed again, this time into a multi-pronged apparatus that hummed with energy. 'Your loved ones would make fascinating test subjects. Human physiology is remarkably resilient, I've discovered that your species could endure significant biological modifications before system failure.'

Something snapped inside Simon. With a roar of fury, he charged at Eradax, the Ring's energy surging through him with unprecedented force, fuelled by his rage and fear.

For a moment, it seemed his attack might succeed. His fist connected with Eradax's chest, the impact creating a visible depression in the alien's metallic form and causing him to stumble a few steps back. But before Simon could press his advantage, Eradax raised his left hand, revealing an iridescent crystal that pulsed with otherworldly light.

'The Gravity Shard,' Eradax said, almost reverently. 'One of my most prized acquisitions.'

The air around Simon distorted, and suddenly it felt as if the weight of the world was pressing down on him. His knees buckled as gravity itself seemed to multiply exponentially, driving him into the rooftop with crushing force. The concrete beneath him cracked under the pressure, forming a shallow crater around his prone form.

Simon struggled against the invisible weight, the Ring's energy fighting to counteract the unnatural gravitational field. But even with its power, he could barely lift his head.

'Impressive resistance,' Eradax noted, increasing the Shard's effect. 'Most beings would have been pulverized by now.'

Pain lanced through Simon's body as the pressure increased, threatening to crush his enhanced form. He could feel the Ring straining to protect him, its energy fluctuating as it battled against a force it had never encountered before.

'This can end now,' Eradax said, standing over him, the Gravity Shard glowing brighter in his hand. 'Remove the Ring, give it to me and this suffering ceases.'

Through gritted teeth, Simon managed a defiant response: 'Never.'

Eradax sighed—a strangely human gesture from the alien being. 'A pity. Your resilience would be admirable in other circumstances.' The pressure increased again, drawing a grunt of pain from Simon as the concrete beneath him continued to fracture.

'Consider this demonstration a preview,' Eradax continued, his voice devoid of emotion. 'What you feel now is but a fraction of what I could inflict upon those you care for. Your parents. Your Layla. All the fragile humans whose lives intersect with yours.'

Simon struggled to move, to speak, to fight back—but the crushing gravity held him immobile. The Ring's power, usually so reliable, couldn't overcome the fundamental force being manipulated against him.

'I will leave you to contemplate your options,' Eradax said, maintaining the Shard's effect at a level that kept Simon immobilized but conscious. 'The Ring for their safety. A simple exchange. I am a collector, Simon Jones, not a destroyer. But make no mistake—I will have what I came for, by whatever means necessary.'

Eradax remained standing over Simon, the Gravity Shard pulsing in his hand as he continued to press Simon into the shattered concrete. Simon remained on his hands and knees, gasping for breath, his body aching from the unnatural force being exerted upon it.

Simon, the Ring's voice was concerned in his mind. *We need to find a way out of this.*

But even as the Ring spoke, Simon knew they faced an impossible situation. Eradax had found him. Identified him. Threatened those he loved most. And demonstrated power beyond anything Simon had encountered before.

For the first time since bonding with the Ring, Simon felt truly vulnerable. Not just for himself, but for everyone connected to him. The casual way Eradax had spoken of using Layla as a test subject chilled him to the core.

He struggled against the crushing force, his body still fighting both the effects of the Gravity Shard and the lingering injuries from his earlier battle. The night that had begun with a quiet dinner had spiralled into a nightmare—one that now threatened to engulf not just him, but everyone he cared about.

And the worst part was staring up at Eradax's impassive face, knowing that the alien would not hesitate to carry out his threats.

The hunter had his prey pinned, and was in no hurry to conclude their confrontation.

CHAPTER 20

The crushing pressure of the Gravity Shard kept Simon pinned to the rooftop, unable to move beyond the shallow breaths that his compressed lungs allowed. Eradax loomed above him, the iridescent crystal pulsing in his metallic hand as he waited for Simon's decision. The silence stretched between them, broken only by the distant sounds of the city and Simon's laboured breathing.

Simon, you cannot surrender me, the Ring's voice echoed in his mind, urgent and concerned. *The consequences would be catastrophic.*

What choice do I have? Simon thought back, his mind racing through scenarios, each more desperate than the last. *He knows who I am. He knows about Layla, my mother ... everyone.*

We can find another way. We've faced impossible odds before.

But this was different. Simon had faced criminals, terrorists, a rival Ring bearer and even augmented humans like the Reclaimers—but never a being with this level of power, this cold detachment, this absolute certainty in its purpose. And never one who had calculated how exactly they would harm not just him, but everyone he loved.

The image of Layla sitting alone at the Turkish restaurant from earlier flashed through his mind. She'd probably left there by now. Unaware that an alien collector was ready to use her as a "test subject" if Simon refused his demands. The same went for his mother, Sarah, too. Potentially in the dangerous crosshairs of a being who would do whatever it took, however it took.

The weight pressing down on him was nothing compared to the weight of this decision.

He won't stop, Simon realized. *Even if we escape today, he'll come after them. He'll use them to get to me.*

Simon, please, the Ring pleaded. *There must be another solution.*

Simon closed his eyes, feeling the familiar presence of the Ring—his partner for years, through darkness and light, through every battle and quiet moment. The sentient force that had changed his life, given him purpose, shown him what it meant to be a guardian instead of just a vigilante.

'I've made my decision,' Simon said aloud, his voice strained against the gravitational pressure.

Eradax tilted his head slightly. 'A wise choice would be in everyone's interest.'

'If I give you the Ring,' Simon managed, each word an effort, 'you leave Earth. You leave my family, Layla, everyone I know untouched. You never return.'

The alien collector considered him for a moment, his crimson eyes unreadable. 'The Ring is my only interest on this primitive world. Once acquired, I have no reason to linger.'

'Swear it,' Simon demanded with what little authority he could muster from his position.

'I do not require oaths to honour agreements,' Eradax replied. 'But if it eases your surrender—yes. I will depart this planet and leave your associations undisturbed once the Ring is mine.'

Simon, don't do this, the Ring implored. *He cannot be trusted.*

I'm sorry, Simon thought back, a profound sadness washing over him. *I can't risk their lives. This looks to be the only way.*

With immense effort, Simon raised his right hand slightly against the crushing gravity. 'Release the pressure enough for me to remove it,' he said to Eradax.

The alien adjusted the Gravity Shard, easing the pressure just enough for Simon to move his arm more freely, though still keeping him firmly pinned to the rooftop.

Simon looked at the silver band on his finger, the runes etched into its surface faintly luminous in the darkness. For years, it had been part of him—more than a tool or weapon, a constant companion through the darkest moments of his life.

I would never do this if there were any other way, he communicated to the Ring. *You know that.*

I know, the Ring responded, its mental voice heavy with resignation. *But are you certain this is the only path?*

Simon thought of Layla waiting for him, of his mother who had already sacrificed so much, of a city that needed protection but not at the cost of innocent lives used as leverage.

Yes, he answered simply. *I'm sure.*

With a deep breath, Simon grasped the Ring between his thumb and forefinger. For a moment, it seemed to resist, clinging to his skin as if reluctant to be parted from him. Then, with a gentle tug, it slipped free.

The effect was immediate and profound. The protective covering that had become his second skin melted away, leaving him in his civilian clothes. The enhanced strength, the heightened senses, the connection to something greater than himself—all vanished in an instant. For the first time in years, Simon Jones was just Simon Jones again.

He felt smaller. Vulnerable. Incomplete.

Holding the Ring in his palm, he extended his hand towards Eradax, his heart breaking with each inch of distance between himself and the artefact that had defined much of his existence for so long.

'Take it,' he said, his voice barely above a whisper. 'And keep your word.'

Eradax deactivated the Gravity Shard, the crushing pressure finally relenting. Simon gasped as his lungs expanded fully, air rushing in to fill the space that had been compressed for so long. The alien reached down with his free hand, plucking the Ring from Simon's palm with surprising delicacy.

'A fine specimen,' Eradax said, raising the Ring to examine it in the dim light. The runes seemed to pulse faintly, as if in protest at being handled by this new bearer. 'Perhaps the finest example of a Fallen Ring I'll ever collect.'

Simon pushed himself to his knees, his body aching from the battle and the gravitational assault. Without the Ring's healing power, every bruise and strain made itself known with sharp clarity.

'This will make a magnificent addition to my collection,' Eradax continued, seemingly oblivious to Simon's suffering as he turned the Ring in his metallic fingers. 'When I acquire the remaining artefacts I seek, my collection will finally be complete. Not merely the achievement of an ancient being who has lived for hundreds of thousands of years—but the ascension of a god!'

The collector's crimson eyes gleamed with a fervour that hadn't been present during their confrontation—something almost religious in its intensity. Simon realized with a chill that he wasn't dealing with just a collector, but a zealot pursuing godhood through acquisition.

'Our transaction is complete,' Eradax said, tucking the Ring into a compartment in his armoured chest. Then, without warning, he backhanded Simon with casual force, sending him sprawling across the rooftop.

'For your troubles,' the alien added dispassionately. 'Consider it a reminder of the natural order between our kinds.'

Blood welling from his split lip, Simon watched as Eradax turned and began walking away across the rooftop, his towering form silhouetted against London's nighttime skyline. The collector had what he wanted. Earth held nothing more of interest to him now.

Simon's vision blurred, darkness creeping in at the edges as consciousness began to slip away. The combined trauma of the fight, the gravitational assault, and the final blow—all without the Ring's protection—was too much for his now-ordinary human body to withstand.

As his awareness faded, Simon felt himself falling, not into unconsciousness, but somewhere else entirely. The rooftop, Eradax, London itself—all dissolved around him like mist in the morning sun.

***

Simon opened his eyes to an impossible vista.

An azure sky stretched endlessly above him, deeper and more vibrant than any Earthly blue. Beneath his feet was not the grimy rooftop of London but polished marble that gleamed with an inner light. In the distance rose graceful columns and elegant structures that might have been plucked from ancient Greece, yet were somehow more perfect, more idealized than any human architecture could achieve.

Time seemed to move differently here—the air itself felt thick with possibility, as if each moment stretched into eternity. Simon blinked, trying to orient himself in this dreamlike realm.

Brilliant light flooded his vision suddenly, ethereal and warm. When it receded, a figure stood before him that made his heart leap in his chest.

Cornelius.

The Superlunary being wore flowing robes of midnight blue embroidered with silver patterns that seemed to shift and change when not directly observed. His immaculate dark hair was slicked back just as Simon remembered, framing features that radiated both wisdom and kindness. He hadn't aged a day since their last meeting—though for a being of his nature, time held different meaning altogether.

A smile illuminated Cornelius's features as he regarded Simon, his eyes reflecting the same mentor-like affection they had years ago.

Without thinking, without hesitation, Simon rushed forward to greet his old friend and teacher. The creator of the Fallen Rings. The being who had guided him after he discovered the power and responsibility that came with the artefact.

'Cornelius,' Simon said, his voice thick with emotion. 'I wasn't sure if I'd see you again.'

The Superlunary's smile widened. 'Did you think I would abandon my favourite Ring-bearer so easily, Simon Jones?'

Simon looked around at the ethereal landscape, then back to Cornelius. 'Am I ... dead?' he asked hesitantly.

Cornelius laughed, the sound like distant chimes carried on a gentle breeze. 'No, my friend. Far from it. You stand at a profound juncture—a crossroads of destiny, if you will.'

He gestured for Simon to walk with him, and as they moved across the shimmering marble, the landscape shifted subtly around them, revealing new vistas with each step.

'You have two paths before you now,' Cornelius continued. 'You could choose to let go of your mortal existence, to join us here among the Superlunary Ones. It is an honour rarely offered, but you have proven yourself worthy many times over.'

Simon's breath caught at the implication. To become like Cornelius—a being beyond time and space. Beyond the mortal limitations. The idea was both terrifying and fascinating.

'Or?' Simon asked, sensing there was more.

Cornelius stopped walking, turning to face Simon directly. 'Or you can return and realize your true power. The power that has always been within you.'

'But I gave up the Ring,' Simon said, confusion etching his features. 'Eradax has it now.'

'You surrendered the physical artefact, yes,' Cornelius nodded. 'But you misunderstand the nature of your relationship with it. The Fallen Ring is not merely a tool that grants abilities to its wearer, Simon. It forms a bond—and yours has grown deeper than almost any I have witnessed throughout the ages.'

He placed a hand on Simon's shoulder, his touch both weightless and profoundly present. 'You are not nothing without the Ring, Simon. Rather, a good portion of your willpower and personality bolster the Ring's abilities. It is as much shaped by you as you are by it.'

Memories flashed through Simon's mind—the moment years ago when he had faced another Ring-bearer, when he had reached a new level of power that had surprised even him. The times when his determination had pushed the Ring's capabilities beyond what seemed possible.

'Remember when you overcame Viktor Nemesis?' Cornelius asked, seemingly reading Simon's thoughts. 'That wasn't just the Ring's power—it was yours as well, channelled through the ancient conduit.'

'But how can I access that power without the Ring?' Simon asked.

'The physical connection has been severed, but the metaphysical bond remains,' Cornelius explained. 'In this moment, you can return to your body and finish your battle against Eradax. You need only awaken and unleash what has always been within you. Reach a new height of your potential.'

Simon fell silent, weighing the options before him. To become a Superlunary—to transcend the limitations of humanity, to join beings of incredible power and knowledge ... The thought was tempting. No more pain, no more struggling against impossible odds.

But then he thought of Layla, worry probably etched across her face by now. His mother, who had stood by him through everything. Friends, colleagues, the city he had sworn to protect. The unwritten chapters of his life that he had yet to experience. Love, growth, the countless small moments that made a human life worth living.

'I can't leave them,' Simon said finally, his voice firm with conviction. 'I can't leave my life behind, not yet. There's too much I still want to experience, too many people who need me.'

Cornelius's smile returned, pride evident in his eyes. 'I knew what choice you would make, Simon Jones. It is why the Ring chose you in the first place. Your heart has always been your greatest strength.'

He stepped back, his form beginning to shimmer with increasing brilliance. 'Return now. Face Eradax. Show him what a true Ring-bearer is capable of. Reclaim what is yours.'

'Will I see you again?' Simon asked, raising a hand to shield his eyes from the intensifying light.

'We will meet again, when the time is right,' Cornelius assured him, his voice already sounding distant. 'There are many meetings and rewards that await you, but for now, go and write those unwritten chapters of your life, Simon. Make them worthy of the man you have become.'

The light grew blinding, engulfing everything around them. Simon felt himself falling upward, if such a thing were possible—being drawn back to his body, back to the rooftop where Eradax still stood with his stolen prize.

Back to the battle that was far from over.

As the ethereal realm faded around him, Simon heard Cornelius's final words: 'Remember, the power was never in the Ring alone. It was also in you.'

The heavenly light consumed his vision entirely, and Simon Jones prepared to make his stand.

Chapter 21

Simon's eyes snapped open, the ethereal realm of the Superlunary Ones fading like a dream upon waking. He found himself exactly where he had fallen—sprawled across the rooftop, the taste of blood on his lips from Eradax's backhanded blow. The alien collector was walking away, his towering form silhouetted against the city lights, the Fallen Ring safely secured within his metallic chest compartment.

Barely seconds had passed in the physical world, yet everything had changed.

Simon pushed himself up from the ground, his movements no longer hindered by pain or exhaustion. Cornelius's words echoed in his mind, igniting something deep within him that had always been there, dormant and waiting.

No, he thought with sudden, unwavering certainty. *I didn't come this far only to see things pan out this way. This is not how the story ends.*

Something primal and powerful surged through his veins—not the familiar energy of the Ring, but something more fundamental. His own inner strength, his own power, amplified and unleashed by the knowledge Cornelius had imparted.

Simon's eyes ignited with brilliant violet-purple light, so intense that it cast shadows across the rooftop. Energy began to radiate from his body in pulsing waves, raw and unfiltered, cracking the concrete beneath his feet and sending ripples through the air itself.

The disturbance caught Eradax's attention. The alien collector stopped and turned, his crimson eyes widening at the sight before him.

'Impossible,' Eradax said, genuine shock breaking through his usual clinical detachment. 'What is this power? You are merely human!'

Simon didn't answer with words. Instead, he raised his right hand, palm outward, fingers splayed. His eyes narrowed in concentration as he focused on what he wanted—what was rightfully his.

Within Eradax's chest compartment, the Fallen Ring began to vibrate, then to glow with the same intense purple light that emanated from Simon's eyes. The metal around it groaned and then tore open as the Ring responded to its true bearer's call, ripping itself free from Eradax's body.

The alien staggered backwards, his metallic hands clutching at the jagged hole in his chest, surprise and pain registering on his face for the first time. 'No! The artefact is mine!'

The Ring shot through the air like a bullet, trailing violet light as it homed in on Simon. It slipped onto his middle finger as if it had never left, the reunion sending a surge of power through Simon's body that made the previous display seem tame by comparison.

In an instant, the familiar transformation took place—but different this time. More complete. More refined. The Guardian emerged, but evolved into something sleeker, more formidable. The dark purple covering flowed over Simon's body, but now interlaced with currents of brilliant energy that pulsed beneath the surface like veins of living light.

Eradax recovered his composure quickly, raising the Gravity Shard which pulsed with iridescent energy. 'This ends now,' he snarled, activating the artefact's power.

The air around Simon distorted as gravity intensified exponentially, enough force to flatten any ordinary being into paste. But Simon stood firm, the enhanced power flowing through him countering the gravitational assault. Each step forward was deliberate and measured as he advanced on Eradax, the concrete beneath him splintering under the competing forces.

'Not possible,' Eradax hissed, pouring more power into the Shard. 'No being can resist the Gravity Shard at full capacity!'

Simon's voice, when he spoke, resonated with newfound authority. 'I'm not just any being.'

With a burst of speed that defied the crushing gravity, Simon closed the distance between them. His hand shot out, grabbing Eradax's wrist and squeezing until the alien's metallic bones creaked under the pressure. The Gravity Shard fell from Eradax's grip, and before it could hit the ground, Simon caught it with his free hand.

'This doesn't belong to you either,' he said, before closing his fist around the Shard.

The artefact cracked, then shattered in Simon's grasp, releasing a blinding flash of energy that knocked Eradax backwards through the air. The alien crashed into an adjacent building, creating a crater in the concrete wall from the impact.

Eradax pulled himself from the wreckage, his crimson eyes now burning with malice rather than clinical interest. His right arm transformed, reshaping into a cannon that glowed with yellow energy.

'You have no concept of what you're interfering with,' Eradax growled. 'The collection must be completed. It is my destiny!'

A scorching yellow streak erupted from the cannon, cutting through the night air towards Simon. The Guardian didn't dodge. Instead, he met the beam with his own blast of purple energy, the two forces colliding in a spectacular display that lit up the London skyline like daybreak.

Windows shattered in nearby buildings as the shockwave radiated outward. The battle was no longer contained, no longer discreet. Despite his enhanced power, Simon realized he needed to end this quickly before more innocent lives were endangered.

Eradax charged forward, his cannon still blazing, his left arm transforming into a blade that gleamed in the harsh light of their energy collision. Simon parried the blade with a forearm hardened by the Ring's power, sparks flying from the impact.

'You're outmatched,' Simon stated, not as a boast but as a simple fact. 'Stand down. Leave this planet. Find your artefacts elsewhere.'

'Never!' Eradax roared, all pretence of cold collection abandoned in the face of Simon's unexpected power. 'I have searched too long, come too far!'

The alien's attacks grew more frenzied, more desperate. Each swing of his blade, each blast from his cannon was met and countered by Simon, whose movements had transcended his previous capabilities. He was operating on a new level—what Cornelius might have called his Omega level.

As they fought across the rooftops of London, Simon could see the first flashing lights of emergency vehicles responding to the disturbance. Time was running out before this battle became a global public spectacle.

With a decisive move, Simon feinted left, drawing Eradax's blade arm wide, then formed his own hands into piercing purple blades of energy. With blinding speed, he drove both blades deep into Eradax's torso, the searing energy cutting through the alien's metallic body like it was paper.

Eradax's fiery eyes widened in shock and torment, his body going rigid as the energy blades disrupted his internal systems. A sharp, metallic screech tore from his throat, echoing around them.

'Your reign of terror ends here,' Simon declared, his voice carrying the weight of absolute certainty. 'It's time I show you just how powerful I really am!'

With a final surge of strength, Simon wrenched his blades upwards, tearing through Eradax's body and separating the alien's head from his shoulders in a clean, devastating strike. Grotesque and decapitated, Eradax's body staggered forward a final step before collapsing to the rooftop with a thunderous impact.

The crimson light in the severed head's eyes flickered, then faded to darkness.

Simon stepped back, his energy blades dissolving as he took in the sight of his fallen enemy. With a deep, primal roar, he released the tension and fury that had built up within him, sending a final pulse of energy skyward where it dissipated harmlessly in the atmosphere.

Gradually, the violet glow surrounding him dimmed to a more controlled level. The battle was over. Eradax, the Collector of Relics, had been defeated.

Sirens wailed from all directions now. Police vehicles, ambulances, fire trucks—all converging on the area. In the distance, Simon could make out the distinctive black vehicles that suggested MI5 involvement. News helicopters were already circling, their spotlights sweeping across the rooftops in search of the source of the disturbance.

Simon glanced down at the Ring on his finger, feeling its familiar presence, but now with a deeper understanding of their connection. It hadn't just been the Ring granting him power—it had also been his own inner strength, amplified and channelled through the ancient artefact.

With one last look at Eradax's fallen form, Simon decided it was time to make himself scarce. The authorities wouldn't only have questions he couldn't answer, but also would want his identity and to experiment on him among countless other investigations and compromising procedures. On top of that, the media attention would only complicate his already complex life.

As blue and red lights illuminated the surrounding buildings and the whir of helicopter blades grew louder, the Guardian slipped away into the shadows, leaving behind the body of an alien collector whose grand ambitions had met their end on a London rooftop.

The night had more challenges ahead—explaining his absence to Layla, dealing with the aftermath of this confrontation, contemplating the revelations Cornelius had shared. But for now, Simon had reclaimed not just his Ring, but a deeper understanding of himself.

And that was a victory that transcended even Eradax's defeat.

CHAPTER 22

The Saturday afternoon crowd flowed around Simon like water around a stone as he stood in the centre of Piccadilly Circus, watching the massive electronic billboards cycle through their advertisements. Tourists snapped photos of the iconic Eros statue while locals hurried by without paying much attention. Normality in all its mundane glory—a stark contrast to the events of just twelve days ago.

Simon sipped his coffee, his gaze occasionally drifting to the news ticker scrolling across one of the screens. Though the headlines had changed over the past two weeks, the mysterious "atmospheric disturbance" over East London still featured prominently in the cycle.

"GOVERNMENT SCIENTISTS DISMISS ALIEN INVASION THEORIES," the ticker proclaimed, followed by "PM ASSURES PUBLIC: NO EVIDENCE OF EXTRATERRESTRIAL INVOLVEMENT IN LONDON LIGHT SHOW."

They've been quite creative with their explanations, the Ring commented in Simon's mind, its mental voice tinged with amusement.

Everything from solar flares to experimental military tech, Simon replied silently. *Anything but the truth.*

The truth, of course, was far less palatable for public consumption: an alien collector had battled a local vigilante across the London skyline, culminating in a confrontation that had shattered windows for blocks and left a headless metallic corpse on a rooftop in East London.

A corpse that had mysteriously disappeared before dawn, along with all evidence of Eradax's existence. MI5, most likely, though Simon couldn't be certain. What he did know was that dark-suited individuals had been systematically interviewing residents in the affected areas, collecting footage, and generally doing what governments do when confronted with the inexplicable—contain, control, and classify.

Do you think they believe any of it? Simon asked, watching a group of teenagers nearby excitedly discussing some new Guardian conspiracy theory, complete with animated hand gestures mimicking energy blasts.

Humans believe what makes them comfortable, the Ring responded. *For most, that means terrestrial explanations. For others, the extraordinary is more appealing than the mundane.*

Simon nodded slightly, moving away from the statue to avoid a large tour group. The past two weeks had been a period of recovery and reflection. Physically, he had healed quickly thanks to the Ring, but mentally, the confrontation with Eradax had left its mark. The revelation from Cornelius about the true nature of his power, the experience of briefly losing the Ring, the brutal end to the alien collector—all of it had reshaped Simon's understanding of himself and his role as the Guardian.

He had kept an intentionally low profile since that night, avoiding any Guardian appearances. Partly to let the public furore die down, partly to process everything that had happened. But the city had been relatively quiet anyway, as if the criminal element had sensed the shift in the atmosphere and decided to lie low for a while too.

We should resume our patrols soon, the Ring suggested, sensing the direction of Simon's thoughts. *The Reclaimers may be back in prison, and Eradax may be gone, but the city still needs protection.*

I know, Simon acknowledged. *Just needed some time to ... adjust.*

The adjustment wasn't just to the events themselves, but to the new equilibrium he had found with the Ring. Since the battle, their connection had deepened in ways Simon was still exploring. His awareness of the Ring's presence was sharper, its communication clearer. The power that flowed between them moved with greater harmony, as if some unseen barrier had been removed.

His phone vibrated in his pocket, pulling him from his reflections. A text from Layla:

Just arrived at Piccadilly. Where are you?

Simon smiled, typing a quick response: *By the big Coca-Cola sign. Black puffer jacket.*

He pocketed his phone and finished his coffee, scanning the crowd for Layla's familiar form. Their relationship had entered a bit of uncertain territory after he'd abruptly left the restaurant that night. The promise to explain everything—the promise interrupted by Eradax's machinations—still hung between them.

Today was the day he would fulfil that promise.

Are you certain about this? the Ring asked, a note of concern in its mental voice.

Yes, Simon replied without hesitation. *After everything that's happened ... I can't keep this part of my life separate from her anymore. It's not fair to either of us.*

The knowledge places her at risk.

So does not knowing, Simon countered. *Besides, if Eradax could figure out who I am, others might too. Better she knows what we're facing than be blindsided.*

Before the Ring could respond, Simon spotted Layla weaving through the crowd towards him. She wore a burgundy coat over a simple white turtleneck top and jeans, her chestnut hair loose around her shoulders. Even in the bustling crowd of Piccadilly, she stood out to him like a beacon.

'Hey,' she said as she reached him, stretching up to kiss his cheek. 'Sorry I'm late. Northern Line was a nightmare.'

'When isn't it?' Simon replied with a smile, taking her hand naturally. 'Thanks for meeting me here.'

'Well, you sounded serious on the phone,' she said, studying his face with those perceptive eyes that missed very little. 'Everything okay?'

Simon hesitated, suddenly aware of how difficult this conversation would be, despite his preparation. 'Yes and no. But definitely not something to discuss in the middle of Piccadilly Circus.'

Layla raised an eyebrow. 'Now I'm intrigued. And slightly concerned.'

'It's nothing bad,' Simon assured her quickly. 'At least, I hope you won't think it is. It's just ... complicated.'

'Simon Jones, master of understatement,' she teased, but her expression remained serious. 'Where did you want to go?'

He considered for a moment. 'My family's house in Brent? My mum and sister are out for the day. It's private, secure.'

'Lead the way,' she said, squeezing his hand.

As they walked towards the Underground station, Simon found himself acutely conscious of the silver Ring on his finger, its weight both familiar and momentous. After years of keeping his dual identity secret, of compartmentalizing his life, he was about to bridge those worlds. The thought was both terrifying and liberating.

They travelled in companionable silence for a while, the Tube journey giving Simon time with his thoughts. Layla seemed to sense his preoccupation, giving him space to process whatever he was preparing to share.

Finally, as they exited the station in Brent, she broke the silence. 'You know, whatever it is, you can tell me. We've known each other since university. I'd like to think there's a foundation of trust there.'

Simon looked at her, at the woman who had been part of his life for so long, who knew so much about him and yet nothing of his most important secret.

'There is,' he said firmly. 'That's why I want to tell you ... everything. No more half-truths or sudden disappearances. No more mysteries.'

They arrived at the modest two-story home where Simon not only grew up, but also still lived in. He unlocked the door, confirming the house was indeed empty.

'Mum and Tessa are at that craft fair in Hampstead,' he explained as he led Layla inside. 'They won't be back until evening.'

They made their way upstairs to Simon's bedroom. He closed the door behind them, despite the empty house, the action symbolic of the privacy this conversation required.

Layla turned to face him, her expression open but guarded.

'This is about why you left the restaurant that night, isn't it?' she asked. 'And all the other times you've suddenly had to go. The odd injuries you try to hide. The way you react when the Guardian is mentioned on the news.'

Simon blinked, surprised at her directness. 'You've noticed all that?'

A small smile curved her lips. 'Simon, I'm observant, not oblivious. I've known something was up for ages. I just ... respected your privacy enough not to push.'

'And I love you for that,' Simon said, the words slipping out before he could consider them. 'But you deserve to know. It affects you too, especially after recent events.'

'Recent events?' Layla echoed, her brow furrowing. 'You mean the light show over East London? What does that have to do with anything?'

Simon took a deep breath, suddenly certain that bringing her here had been the right decision. The security of his home, the privacy it afforded—this was the perfect place for what he needed to reveal.

'What I'm about to tell you—and show you—will change everything,' he said, his voice steady despite his racing heart. 'Are you sure you're ready for that?'

Layla studied him for a long moment, something like realization dawning in her eyes. Then, with a slow nod: 'I'm ready, Simon. No more secrets between us.'

As Simon prepared to reveal the truth he'd kept hidden for so long, he felt a curious mixture of dread and relief. The moment of truth had arrived—a revelation that would change their relationship forever, for better or worse.

She already suspects, the Ring observed.

Yes, Simon agreed. *She's always been perceptive.*

Whatever happened next, there would be no going back. But after facing Eradax, after nearly losing the Ring, after discovering the true nature of his power—Simon was done with half-measures and divided lives. If Layla was to be part of his future, she deserved to know all of him, not just the parts he felt safe revealing.

The Guardian's identity would remain secret from the world at large, but to Layla, Simon would finally be whole.

CHAPTER 23

S imon stood in the centre of his bedroom, the familiar surroundings a stark contrast to the extraordinary conversation he was about to initiate.

Layla sat on the edge of his bed, patient but expectant, her eyes never leaving his face.

'I've been trying to figure out how to tell you this for years,' Simon began, his voice steady despite the nervousness fluttering in his chest. 'Every time I thought I was ready, something would hold me back—fear, mostly. Fear of how it would change things between us. Fear of putting you at risk.'

'Simon,' Layla said gently, 'whatever it is, just say it. It's still you.'

He took a deep breath. 'By day I'm Simon Jones, but at night, I'm the one who protects the city. The vigilante.'

A moment of silence stretched between them as understanding dawned in Layla's eyes. 'You're saying ... ' She trailed off, the implication too extraordinary to voice.

Instead of answering with words, Simon raised his right hand, displaying the silver ring that had adorned his middle finger for years. The runes etched into its surface began to glow faintly, pulsing with a gentle violet light.

'This is the Fallen Ring,' he explained. 'It chose me, bonded with me. And together, we became the Guardian.'

Layla stared at the glowing ring, her expression a mixture of disbelief and dawning comprehension. 'All this time,' she whispered. 'All those sudden disappearances, the unexplained injuries, the way you always seemed to know about incidents before they hit the news ...'

Simon nodded. 'I wanted to tell you so many times. But the more people who know, the more dangerous it becomes—for them and for me.'

'Show me,' Layla said suddenly, her voice firmer. 'I need to see it.'

Simon hesitated only briefly before stepping back to give himself space. He closed his eyes, feeling the familiar connection with the Ring deepen as he allowed the transformation to begin. This time, he controlled it more carefully than usual, slowing the process so Layla could witness the change.

The silver band on his finger seemed to melt, flowing like liquid metal up his arm and across his body. The dark purple covering enveloped him inch by inch, the transformation accompanied by a soft violet glow that illuminated the bedroom in ethereal light. As the metamorphosis completed, Simon stood before Layla as the Guardian, his eyes now radiating that distinctive purple brilliance that had become his signature in London's night sky.

Layla rose slowly from the bed, her mouth slightly open in astonishment. She approached him cautiously, as if afraid he might disappear if she moved too quickly. When she stood before him, she raised a tentative hand and touched his shoulder, feeling the strange material that was neither fabric nor skin, but something altogether different.

'This is …' She shook her head, words failing her. 'It's really you in there?'

'It's me,' Simon confirmed, his voice carrying a subtle resonance in this form. 'The Ring enhances what's already there—strength, speed, senses. But it's still me underneath.'

With another thought, Simon allowed the transformation to reverse, the purple covering receding back into the Ring until he stood before her as himself again, dressed in his tech fleece tracksuit.

'That was …' Layla exhaled slowly, processing what she'd witnessed. Then, unexpectedly, a smile spread across her face, and a playful glint appeared in her eyes. 'You know, this is like something out of a film. Who'd have thought it? I'm in a relationship with a superhero?'

The tension in Simon's shoulders eased at her reaction. Of all the scenarios he'd imagined, this accepting, almost amused response hadn't been one of them.

'Not exactly how I'd describe myself,' he said with a small laugh.

'What would you call it then?' Layla asked, leading him to sit beside her on the bed.

Simon considered this. 'A guardian. Someone who protects those who can't protect themselves. Someone who helps those in need. My beginning as the Guardian was not glamorous. But since then, I've evolved into … a symbol, I guess.'

For the next hour, Simon told her a lot—how he'd discovered the Ring, his early days learning to control its powers, the nocturnal escapades that had earned him the Guardian moniker in London's streets. He spoke of battles with criminals, rescues from burning buildings, confrontations with other enhanced individuals. With each story, Layla listened intently, asking questions, filling in gaps in her understanding of the man she thought she'd known completely.

'And that night at the restaurant,' she said finally. 'When you left so suddenly. That was because of … him? The alien collector you mentioned?'

Simon nodded. 'Eradax. He'd set a trap using the criminals I'd put away—the ones who broke out of Belmarsh. They were bait to draw me out, to test my capabilities. And then Eradax himself appeared.'

'The light show over East London,' Layla murmured. 'That was you fighting him?'

'Yes. It was the closest I've ever come to …' Simon didn't finish the sentence, but he didn't need to. The implication was clear.

Layla was quiet for a moment, absorbing everything. 'Will you keep doing it?' she asked finally. 'Being the Guardian? Indefinitely?'

Simon paused, considering her question carefully. The truth was, the events two weeks ago had made him re-evaluate his priorities. He had come face to face with the consequences of his life as the Guardian; he had even come close to death, and all of it had given him a newfound perspective.

'I think I've had my fair share of epic battles,' he said finally. 'At least for now. I want to focus on other things that matter so much to me. Like you. My family.'

He reached out, taking her hand in his. 'I'm not saying I'll stop completely. There are still people who need help, and I have the ability to provide that help. But balance is important. I've been the Guardian almost every night for years. Maybe it's time to let Simon Jones live a little more.'

Layla squeezed his hand, her eyes soft with understanding. 'I think that sounds reasonable. And for what it's worth, I'm proud of what you've done. All those people you've helped ...'

'You're not scared?' Simon asked. 'Knowing what's out there? What I've faced?'

'Terrified,' she admitted with a small laugh. 'But also reassured, knowing you're out there. And now that I know, you don't have to carry this alone anymore.'

The weight that had been pressing on Simon's chest for years seemed to lift at her words. The secret he'd guarded so carefully had finally been shared, and instead of driving them apart, it had brought them closer.

'How about we go get that dinner we missed two weeks ago?' he suggested. 'No interruptions this time. I promise.'

'I'd like that,' Layla smiled, rising from the bed. 'I know a great Turkish place in Green Lanes.'

Simon laughed. 'Maybe somewhere different. For variety's sake.'

As they prepared to leave, Simon caught himself thinking about the future—a future that suddenly seemed brighter and more certain than it had in years. He imagined family gatherings where he wouldn't have to keep checking his phone for emergency alerts, nights spent with Layla without the constant worry of having to disappear mysteriously.

And soon, an elegant ring for Layla, the one he'd propose with.

You could always get her a Fallen Ring, the Ring suggested in his mind, its mental voice carrying a hint of what might have been humour. *I hear they're quite rare and valuable.*

I think you need to work on your comedy, Simon replied silently, a smile playing at his lips despite himself.

Thousands of years old and still learning, the Ring retorted. *But ... I am more than pleased for you, Simon.*

As they left the house, Simon felt a sense of balance he hadn't experienced in years. The Guardian would still protect London's streets, still face whatever threats emerged from the darkness. But Simon Jones would live too—fully and completely, without shadows and half-truths obscuring his relationships.

It wasn't an ending, but rather a new beginning. A chapter where heroism and humanity could coexist, neither sacrificed for the other. And for now, that was enough.

Chapter 24

The cell in HMP Wakefield was exactly three paces wide and four paces long. Dushane had counted them countless times over the three weeks since his transfer to what the prison system officially termed a "High Security Estate" but what inmates simply called "Monster Mansion." Reserved for the most dangerous criminals in the UK, it was a far cry from Belmarsh—both in security measures and in isolation.

Dushane rotated his shoulder carefully, wincing as the familiar ache radiated down his arm. The doctors had reset the joint after the Guardian had dislocated it, but they hadn't done the best job. Probably because he was a dangerous criminal. Either way, the Guardian had made his message clear: the injury was meant to be remembered.

Through the narrow window of his cell door, Dushane watched the guards escorting another prisoner down the corridor. Every movement in this facility was monitored, every word recorded, every potential weakness identified and eliminated. The lessons of the Belmarsh escape had been learned well.

No one would be breaking out of Wakefield. Not anytime soon.

The heavy steel door to the exercise yard buzzed open, signalling the beginning of their daily hour of outdoor access. Dushane stepped out of his cell, keeping his face neutral as he joined the procession of inmates making their way through the series of checkpoints and reinforced doors that led to the yard.

Callum was already in the yard when Dushane arrived, occupying their usual corner away from most of the other prisoners. The kid had lost weight since their capture, his formerly lean frame now bordering on gaunt. The gleaming confidence that had radiated from him when he wore his electrical suit was gone, replaced by the wary alertness of a man who knew he was out of his depth.

'Boss,' he greeted Dushane with a slight nod, shifting to make room on the bench.

Dushane sat, his eyes scanning the yard for their other companions. 'Wei and Mateo?'

'Isolation,' Callum replied, keeping his voice low. 'Wei got caught with contraband electronics again. Mateo put three enforcers in the infirmary yesterday.'

Dushane sighed. Four of London's most proficient criminals, once equipped with technology that could have made them kings, now reduced to prison yard politics and petty infractions. The mighty Reclaimers, scattered and contained.

'Any word from the outside?' he asked, though he expected little. Their communication channels had been systematically dismantled since their recapture.

Callum shook his head. 'Nothing new. London's quiet. No sign of our ... benefactor.'

Eradax. The alien collector who had given them power beyond imagination, only to use them as pawns in his grand game of acquisition. Dushane had spent many sleepless nights wondering what had become of him after their capture. The news reports about "atmospheric disturbances" over East London had told him enough.

The Guardian and Eradax had faced off, and given that there had been no alien invasion in the days that followed, one of them had lost. Dushane had his suspicions about who the victor had been.

'I don't think we'll be hearing from him again,' Dushane said finally.

Callum looked at him sharply. 'You think he's—'

'Dead? Maybe. Gone? Definitely.' Dushane rotated his shoulder again, feeling the familiar twinge. 'Our usefulness ended the moment we failed him.'

A group of inmates passed by, eyeing them with the calculation of predators assessing potential prey. Since arriving at Wakefield, Dushane and his crew had been forced to establish their position in the hierarchy quickly and violently. Word of their scrap with the Guardian had spread across the prison, earning them a wary respect. But in a place like this, reputation wasn't enough; respect had to be maintained. Hence Mateo's current stay in isolation.

'Still think about it, though,' Callum murmured once the others had passed. 'The tech. The power. What we could have done with more time.'

Dushane felt a familiar anger stirring in his chest. He did think about it—constantly. The weight of the shockwave gauntlets on his wrists. The rush as buildings crumbled before him. The look of fear on the Guardian's face when they'd first ambushed him.

Before it had all gone wrong.

'No point dwelling on it,' he said, keeping his voice level despite the rage simmering beneath. 'That chapter's closed.'

'And the Guardian?' Callum pressed, unable to let it go. 'What about him?'

The Guardian. The purple-eyed vigilante who had put them away twice now, who had somehow turned the tables on Eradax himself if Dushane's suspicions were correct. The being who had intentionally dislocated Dushane's shoulder while promising worse if he ever threatened anyone again.

'What about him?' Dushane countered, though the question sent a fresh wave of hatred through him.

'We still going after him when we get out?' Callum's voice had dropped even lower, barely audible above the general noise of the yard.

'If,' Dushane corrected. 'Not when. If.'

The reality of their situation had settled on Dushane during the endless nights in his cell. The authorities weren't taking chances this time. Multiple life sentences. No possibility of parole. Special monitoring. Regular cell transfers to prevent planning.

The system was ensuring the Reclaimers would never reclaim anything again.

'Still,' Callum persisted, 'if we did get out—'

'I'd kill him with my bare hands given half a chance,' Dushane interrupted, the words coming out before he could stop them. The admission hung in the air between them, raw and honest. 'But I'm not building my life around that fantasy. Not anymore.'

Across the yard, a fight broke out between two inmates, drawing the guards' attention. Dushane watched dispassionately as the scuffle was quickly contained, the participants dragged away for disciplinary action.

'So what then?' Callum asked. 'We just ... exist in here? For decades? Until we die?'

It was the question Dushane had been asking himself since arriving at Wakefield. The answer still eluded him most days.

'For now, we survive,' he replied finally. 'We build new connections. We adapt. We wait.'

'For what?'

Dushane turned to look at the younger man directly. 'For whatever comes next. This isn't the end of our story, Callum. It's just a chapter we didn't plan for.'

The words were meant to be reassuring, but they rang hollow even to Dushane's ears. The truth was more complicated, more bitter. Without their tech, without their freedom, without maintaining their network—they were just four more inmates in a system designed to contain them until death. Though Dushane would never surrender to that fate.

His shoulder throbbed, a sore reminder of his defeat. The Guardian's warning echoed in his mind: "'If you ever

threaten anyone else again, I won't stop at a shoulder.'"
The vigilante had meant it. Dushane had seen it in those
inhuman purple eyes—a line had been drawn, and crossing it would bring consequences far worse than prison.

The yard buzzer sounded, signalling the end of their
outdoor time. As they filed back towards the building,
Dushane caught sight of Wei being escorted from the isolation wing, his expression carefully blank but his eyes
finding Dushane's across the yard. A silent communication passed between them—acknowledgment, solidarity,
shared defeat.

Back in his cell, Dushane resumed his daily ritual of
pacing the confined space. Three steps wide. Four steps
long. Over and over until mealtime. Then more pacing
until lights out. Then dreams of power and vengeance that
dissolved with the morning buzzer.

Yes, he would kill the Guardian if given the chance. He
would savour every moment of it, make the vigilante suffer
for the humiliation he had inflicted. But Dushane was
nothing if not pragmatic. That opportunity might never
come, and building his existence around the fantasy would
only lead to madness.

So for now, he would focus on the immediate. Surviv-
ing each day. Maintaining what influence he could within
these walls. Keeping his crew together despite the system's
attempts to separate them.

And perhaps, in the quiet moments between counts and
meals and exercise, he would allow himself to remember
the feeling of that power—the shockwave gauntlets on his

wrists, the world trembling before him, the name "Reclaimers" spoken with fear and respect.

Just memories now. But memories that kept the ember of hatred burning, even as hope diminished with each passing day.

Dushane rotated his shoulder again, embracing the pain this time rather than wincing from it. Some reminders were useful. Some grudges worth nursing, even if they might never be acted upon.

And some enemies—like the Guardian—were worth remembering, even from the confines of a cell three paces wide and four paces long in a prison designed to hold monsters.

EPILOGUE

The aurora danced across the Himalayan sky, ribbons of iridescent light cascading through the darkness in patterns no human scientist could fully explain. Here, atop the highest peaks where the air grew too thin for most living beings to survive, the veil between worlds thinned. Reality itself seemed more malleable, more willing to reveal its deeper mysteries.

Cornelius stood at the edge of a precipice, wrapped in a thick brown overcoat with fur trim that swayed gently in the cold breeze. He required none of these human accoutrements, of course. As a Superlunary, a being who transcended time and space, physical discomfort was a foreign concept. But he had found over countless millennia that taking human form—embracing its limitations and sensations—provided perspective that pure observation could not.

Beside him stood a younger Superlunary, one who had not long been formed from the ether light. They appeared as a slender figure in simple white robes, their features shifting subtly in the aurora's glow.

'They're so small,' the young one said, gazing down at a distant village nestled in the valley below, lights twinkling like earthbound stars. 'Fragile. Primitive. How can beings so basic and fleeting matter in the cosmic scale?'

Cornelius smiled, patience born of ages reflected in his eyes. 'That very brevity gives them urgency. Purpose. They must search for meaning within limited time, unlike us who measure existence in eons.'

The young Superlunary seemed unconvinced. 'Yet they spend their short lives in conflict. Pursuing wealth. Power. Destroying their own habitat. How can such beings be worthy of our attention?'

'You see only part of the intricate picture,' Cornelius replied, his gaze now fixed on the celestial display above. 'Humanity contains multitudes. For every act of destruction, there is creation. For every moment of cruelty, there is compassion.'

The aurora intensified, colours shifting to deep purples and blues that reminded Cornelius of the Fallen Ring bonded to a certain Londoner. He had been watching that particular human with special interest.

'Consider Simon Jones,' Cornelius said, his voice carrying the weight of a storyteller passing down an important legend.

'The Ring-bearer?' The young one's attention shifted, clearly intrigued despite their scepticism. 'The human you intervened for?'

'The very same,' Cornelius confirmed. 'When the Fallen Ring first found him, he was consumed by rage. His path might easily have led to darkness.'

The aurora pulsed, and within its light, images formed—memories that Cornelius drew forth for his companion to witness. A younger Simon, influenced by the Ring's power and on a war path born from wrath. Early confrontations with criminals often ended with deadly force.

'He was no different from the many who seek power only for vengeance,' the young Superlunary observed.

'At first,' Cornelius agreed. 'But observe what followed.'

The aurora shifted again, displaying Simon's evolution. Learning control. Choosing to protect rather than simply punish. Finding balance between the human and the hero. Building connections—with his family, with Layla, with the city he had sworn to protect.

'He changed,' the young one acknowledged.

'He grew,' Cornelius corrected gently. 'As humans do. In ways we, with our eternal perspective, find profound. They can transform within a single lifetime, one that is a mere fraction of ours.'

The images in the aurora showed Simon's most recent trial—confronting Eradax, sacrificing the Ring to protect those he loved, then discovering the power had also been within him, channelled through the artifact.

'When faced with an entity as ancient and powerful as Eradax, this human not only survived but triumphed,' Cornelius continued. 'Not through sheer strength or superior technology, but through the very qualities that make humanity unique—adaptability, determination, and the capacity for growth.'

The young Superlunary was silent for a moment, absorbing this perspective. 'One exceptional case could not redeem an entire species, could it?'

Cornelius laughed, the sound echoing across the mountain peaks. 'Indeed not! But Simon Jones is not unique in his potential, merely in how circumstances allowed that potential to manifest. Each human carries similar capacity, the deciding factor is in what they choose to do once enlightenment dawns on them.'

He gestured towards the sprawling expanse of the Earth below them. 'That is why we watch. Why we occasionally intervene. Not because humans are perfect, or that they are all destined for greatness, but because they constantly surprise us with what they can become.'

The aurora began to fade as dawn approached, the first rays of sunlight piercing the eastern horizon. Soon the celestial phenomena would retreat, the veil between worlds thickening once more.

'The Cosmic Archive grows richer with each human story,' Cornelius said, his tone reflective. 'Even the briefest lives can teach those of us who exist beyond time, if we are willing to learn.'

'And the Ring-bearer?' the young one asked. 'What becomes of him now?'

Cornelius smiled, glancing down at London where Simon was at this very moment sharing breakfast with Layla, laughing about something ordinary and wonderful. 'His story continues. As do all their stories. And we have the delight to witness how each pan out.'

'Will you intervene again if needed?' There was curiosity in the question, perhaps a hint of the young Superlunary's evolving perspective.

'Perhaps.' Cornelius began to shed his human appearance as the aurora's final lights faded, his form becoming more luminous, less defined. 'But I suspect Simon Jones will continue to surprise us without my help.'

The young Superlunary followed suit, their form dissolving into pure energy. 'I would like to observe more of these humans,' they admitted, their voice now everywhere and nowhere as they shed physical limitation. 'To understand what you see in them.'

'Then you are already wiser than many who have existed far longer,' Cornelius replied, his essence merging with the dawn light. 'The universe reveals its greatest secrets to those willing to look beyond the surface, to those that tread that bit deeper.'

As the sun crested the mountaintops, both the Superlunary Ones departed that plane of existence, returning to realms beyond human comprehension. But part of their awareness remained fixed on Earth—on its struggles and triumphs, its darkness and light.

And in London, the story of the Fallen Ring and its bearer wasn't over. It was merely entering a new chapter, with possibilities as limitless as the universe itself.

AUTHOR'S NOTE

To those who read the early version of *The Fallen Ring* Three—previously titled *Cosmic Crisis*—this is the definitive and fully reimagined edition. The original draft never quite sat right with me. Something about it lacked the creativity, spark, and depth I knew Simon's journey deserved. It didn't explore the kinds of scenarios I had envisioned for him, and ultimately, it just didn't feel like the story I wanted to tell.

This new version? It's a whole different experience. I've taken the time to dive deeper, push boundaries, and finally bring Simon into the moments I always wanted him to live through. I'm genuinely proud of this book—it was a blast to write, and I hope it's just as exciting to read!

Acknowledgements

Books are never one-person endeavours. They take time, patience, and a lot of support behind the scenes. I'm deeply grateful to my editor, to my aunt, and to everyone who encouraged and believed in me along the way. I would also like to thank Dean Wesley Smith; his books are golden insights into the writing process, especially for extremely creative writers. Thank you all for helping bring this story to life. I couldn't have done it without you.

ABOUT THE AUTHOR

Key Dawkins is a writer and author from the UK. Since childhood, he's always wanted to write and publish a book. This is his third one within the young adult and thriller genre, following the first and second *The Fallen Ring* novellas.